MEETING HUGO DANVERS

Pamela Foss

contents

CHAPTER 1

S talking isn't that bad, right? People do it sometimes, even if it's on accident. I did it, it was a mistake, but it didn't matter to me. Murder is worse.

I'm inside a café. There isn't a crowd. A couple of tables are by the window and center, and the walls are covered with paintings and menus.

I sit down at a table near the window. When I hear the cashier call my name, I walk toward the counter. On my way toward the counter, I trip over my own feet. Of course, clumsy dumb me couldn't help but trip.

Before my face can hit the ground, someone grabs my jacket and prevents it from happening.

"Are you alright?" a male voice asks me.

I get back on my feet and look at the man. He has fluffy brown hair with hazel eyes. He has a small bandage on his nose, and it looks cute.

He smiles sweetly at me. I smile back with a nod and say: "Yes, thank you. Good reflexes."

His smile widens, and he puts his hand in his pocket. His other hand has a cup of coffee. "Well, thank you. I'm glad I could help."

There's an awkward silence. He points at the counter. "Coffee?"

I shook my head. "Sorry?"

He chuckles and replies: "You got coffee, right?"

"Oh! Right!" I say. I turn to the counter and get my coffee.

"You're lucky you didn't fall," the cashier tells me. "That would've been a hard hit."

I laugh softly and reply: "Yeah, it would've hurt."

I get my coffee and pay. I turn around, and the man still looks at me. He points at a table. I walk over to it, and so does he.

We sit down at opposite sides. He smiles and says: "I'm Peter Quintin."

I smile back and reply: "John Welling."

We sit in silence for a moment.

"Do you come here often? I have a feeling I've seen you before," Peter asks me. "Your clumsiness is familiar."

I can't help but laugh at his comment. "I'm sorry I'm a disturber of the peace in this café!"

He laughs with me. I take a sip of my coffee. It's hot, and I place it back on the table as I bite my lip. Peter chuckles as he sees me do it.

"I come here every day," I say. "I think I've seen you here before."

He smiles at me and takes a sip of his coffee. He places it down and says: "You're right. The coffee is hot."

I chuckle at his comment.

He checks his watch, and I take it as a sign that he has to leave. He takes a tissue and a pen and writes something down. He tears it off and gives me the piece of paper. "My lunch break is almost over. Here is my number if you would want to meet again."

I smile and take the tissue. "Thank you, Peter."

I take the leftover tissue and write my number on it. Peter takes the paper, looks at it, and smiles.

He stands up, and I do the same. We shake hands with a wide smile. As Peter takes his leaves, I sit back down. This time, I blow before taking a sip of my coffee.

My phone rings. I check who it is. It's my girlfriend, Lily. I press the call button and don't even have the chance to greet her.

"Where the fuck are you?" she asks angrily.

I sigh and answer: "Lily, baby, I'm at the café as usual."

"Come back home!"

She hangs up before I can answer. She sounds mad. I stand up, take my jacket and coffee, and leave the building.

It's a sunny day. It's the middle of June anyway. People wear sunglasses, shorts, hats, shirts, and crop tops. I, on the other hand, wear winter clothes. I wear a nice old sweater with jeans.

People do look weird at me as I pass by. It's hot, and I'm a man in winter clothes.

I don't feel the warmth of the sun. That's one of the reasons why I wear these clothes. The second reason is that I find them comfortable.

I smile and nod at the people I know. They greet me back by doing the same thing. I drink my coffee on my way and throw away the empty cup.

I arrive at my house and get the keys from my pocket. Before I can even place the less in the lock, the door opens. I get pulled inside by Lily.

Her red hair falls nicely down her back. But her eyes, her dark brown eyes, shoot right through me.

She frowns angrily. "The café, huh?"

I nod. "Yes, the café."

She hits me in the face. I step back and touch my cheek as it starts to sting. "Darling?"

She shakes her head. "I'm not your baby, darling, honey, or anything!"

My eyes widen. "What?"

I see three suitcases behind her. Confused, I look at her. "What do you mean?"

A man enters the hallway. He doesn't look familiar. He stands next to Lily and places a hand on her shoulder.

"Get the hint?" Lily asks me.

My eyes widen. I look at the man and back to Lily. She sighs. "You're as stupid as a chicken."

I frown. "What?"

I step back as I realize what's happening. Lily nods. I shake my head. "But...darling..." I say, hoping this isn't true.

I see her form fists. "I am not your darling!"

"I-I did everything I could! I did the groceries, the dishes, cleaned the house, cooked for you, and so on! What did I do to deserve this?"

She shakes her head. "You're a disappointment. A big mistake!"

I go quiet as my heart shatters into a million pieces. All the words I try to say form a cork in the center of my throat. It keeps all the words inside me.

She looks at the man. "Dear, can you take my suitcases to the car?"

He nods with a gentle smile. "Of course."

He takes the suitcases and leaves the house, leaving Lily and me alone in the hallway.

"That's right. I'm leaving you," Lily tells me. "That's Hans. We've been dating for three weeks already."

I frown as anger boils inside me. "How could you?"

She shakes her head and says: "I told you, you're a disappointment."

"HOW COULD YOU!?" I shout. "I did everything a good man could do!"

She hits me in the stomach. "How dare you raise your voice at me!?"

I gasp for air and sink onto the floor.

She sighs and takes her leave. "Asshole."

I hear the car door close. The engine starts. They left me. She left me for that ass.

I sit on the floor for what feels like ages. Finally, tears form in my eyes. I am on my knees, with my head on my thighs. I sob and sob for minutes straight.

I hear a car with sirens outside. A car door opens and shuts. Footsteps approach my doorstep. "Hello?" someone asks.

I hold my breath and try to contain my tears. I form fists with my hand and shut my eyes.

The footsteps approach me. Someone kneels next to me and places a hand on my back. "Sir, are you alright?"

I finally arch my back. I can feel the tears rolling down my cheeks. I take a deep breath before looking to my right.

Both our eyes widen.

Another person approaches us. He stops at the doorstep. "Agent, is everything alright?"

Our eye contact doesn't break. Silence falls upon us.

Tears form in my eyes, and I start sobbing again.

He pulls me in and hugs me tightly. The other cop comes closer and kneels next to us in silence.

"Oh, John...what happened to you?" the man asks.

I pull back from the hug and wipe my tears away in shame. With pain, I smile at the two agents.

"Peter...I didn't expect you to be a cop!" I say a bit too loud. I keep having that smile on my face.

He looks at me with sympathy. "What happened? Your cheek is red, and you're sobbing."

Confused, I look at the other agent. He nods. I touch the cheek Lily hit. "She hit me..." I whisper.

"Who did?" the other cop asks me.

"She left me...for a prick..." I whisper.

I look at my hands. They're trembling. I take a deep breath and stand up. I walk toward the living room but stop at the doorframe. Someone just smashed the broken pieces of my heart with a hammer.

Peter stands beside me and looks as shocked as me at the room.

The couch is torn open, the cupboards are broken, and shattered glass is on the floor.

I look at Peter. "Is there a chance that I can sleep at the police station?"

I gently shake his arm for his attention. He looks at me, still shocked. "Y-yes, we can figure something out."

I smile and go upstairs to get a bag of clothes and other stuff.

I feel light-headed as I go downstairs. My vision blurs as I look at the car. I feel my legs weaken as I step forward.

I get into the car. Everyone's quiet. Peter is in the driver's seat. I see him glance at me through the mirror. I smile at him. He lowers his gaze and starts the engine.

I lean my head against the glass of the window. We pass houses, trees, and people. It doesn't take long before my tiredness takes over. I shut my eyes and drift off to sleep.

Chapter 2

Slowly, I open my eyes. I look around and see nothing that looks like a police station.

I'm lying on a soft dark red couch with circle-shaped pillows. On my left, I see a wide table.

I sit up with a light headache turning my vision black. I rub my eyes and look at the room. It's a cozy living room. There are some plants, paintings, pictures, et cetera.

I stand up and walk toward a picture frame. I see no familiar faces. I look to my right and see a note on the front door.

Confused, I walk toward it.

If you're awake, you can go to the café. I should be there, if not, go to the police station and ask for me. - Peter

So this is Peter's place. Go to the café, it says. I shrug. It doesn't look like I have much choice. I look at the couch and see my bag of clothes. I sigh and change into newer clothes. A black hoodie with grey trousers will do.

The door is unlocked as I try opening it. I step outside and take in the fresh air. A smile tugs at the corners of my mouth.

I shut the door behind me. There's no turning back now.

I look at his house number before leaving. I recognize the street. It won't be too hard to remember his address.

I take another deep breath and go on.

Walking through the streets, I realize how loud it is. I'm used to softly humming as I walk, but now I hear people.

Again, I greet the people I know with a smile.

I arrive at the café. I smile and step inside. I do the usual things. Order coffee, take a seat, and wait for my order.

This time, when I sit down, a man calls my name. It isn't the cashier. I look up to see Peter with a gentle smile. I smile back at him.

"Peter, hey!" I greet him. "How's it going?"

"I'm doing alright!" he says as he sits down. "How are you doing? You had a rough night yesterday."

Now I remember why I was here. I fall silent as I remember yesterday. Lily broke up with me. I lower my gaze as I remember what Peter did.

I can sense his eyes on me, watching me with pity. He places his coffee on the table in silence.

Someone calls my name. I take a deep breath before standing up to get my coffee.

I sigh as I walk back to Peter. With a small smile of pain, I sit back down.

I place my coffee on the table and leave my hands next to it. Peter takes my hand and gently squeezes it. I look up at him.

"How do you feel?" he asks me again.

I shrug. "I don't know. Angry? Sad? Both."

His touch is warm. I smile slightly. He notices and chuckles. I grab my coffee and want to take a sip. Peter stops me by putting a hand over the lid. Confused, I look at him.

He laughs softly. "Have you forgotten what happened yesterday?"

I squint my eyes as I try to remember what happened. I laugh as I remember. Peter laughs and nods. "Yeah, don't do that!"

I chuckle and blow before drinking my coffee. Peter smiles widely, and so do I.

As I drink my coffee, I can't help but notice my gaze going to his lips. His hand stays on mine as we talk. He smiles so sweetly at me. His touch is warmer than a summer's day.

We talk for a minute or fifteen. Peter checks his watch. I don't want him to go.

"Do you need to leave?" I ask him.

He presses his lips together and nods. I force a smile.

"You can stay over at my place," Peter tells me. "Unless there's somewhere else."

"I can stay over at a friend's place," I reply. As much as I'd like to stay with him, I don't want to be a bother to him. He helped me already. "Do you mind bringing my bag to the place? I left it at your place."

He nods. "Of course!" He gives me a tissue and a pen. I wrote down the address and gave it back.

He reads it and smiles. "I'll see you then."

He stands up, and I do the same. We shake hands again, and he leaves.

I watched him leave the café. For some reason, I walked outside a couple of minutes later. I follow Peter from a distance.

When he crosses a street, I do the same. When he stops, I hide. He doesn't seem to notice me. He drinks his coffee and throws away the cup in a bin. I watch his every movement.

We arrive at the police station. Peter enters, and I stay behind. I sit on a bench a couple of buildings away. I take out my phone and text my friend, Jackson Smith.

10:36 - JohnHey, Jackie! Is it possible for me to stay over at your place?

I shut my phone and put it back in my pocket. I watch the doors of the police station for signs of Peter. My phone buzzes.

10:37 - JacksonHey, mate! Of course! Is there a reason?

I sigh and think of an answer. I stay quiet as I think of a reply.

10:40 - JohnYeah, Lily and I broke up. She destroyed my whole place.

10:41 - Jackson She what!? I'm sorry to hear that. Of course, you can stay over. When will you be here?

10:41 - JohnI'll be coming in a couple of hours. I have to do something first.

He stays silent, and I take it as an agreement. He'll be ready when I arrive. I look at the police station again.

Peter leaves the building with another agent. Peter is wearing something else. Instead of a plain white shirt and black trousers, he's wearing police clothes.

I stare at them as they walk my way. I stand up and pretend to look at a shop's sunglasses. I try a pair and look at the mirror and see their reflection.

As they pass by, I quit what I'm doing and follow from a distance. They don't notice me. It looks like they're patrolling.

A little girl runs over to them. She seems sad. She tugs at the other cop's pants. Peter gives the girl a sweet smile and says something. He wipes away the girl's tears with his thumb and caresses her cheek. He's so gentle with her.

I see him tell the girl more things. The girl's sobs lessen as a small smile appears. Peter's smile widens, and he stands up, taking the girl's hand.

He nods at the other cop, and he smiles in response. I sense that the little girl is lost.

Peter looks back at the girl and smiles widely. The three cross the street and walk toward me. I hide away in a nearby alley. They pass by me. The girl saw me.

"What's going on?" I hear someone ask.

"There was a man!" I hear the girl say.

I hide away behind a trash can. As I hear footsteps, I hold my breath, put on my hood, and turn my face away.

"I see no one here," I hear Peter say. He's right next to me. "Hello?"

I hold my breath and start to feel dizzy. I've been holding my breath for a minute already. I hear footsteps again, but they fade away.

"There's no one. It's okay," Peter tells the girl. "Shall we get some candy for you? We'll find your father."

Their voices fade away. I gasp for air. Finally, I can breathe again. I lean against the wall as I take deep breaths.

That was close, too close.

I stand up when I think I'll be fine. I walk out of the alley. It doesn't even matter that I lost Peter and the other two. I walk at a fast pace to Jackson's place.

When I arrive, I knock on his door. I take a deep breath to calm myself down. Jackson opens the door. He's slightly taller than me and has blonde hair and green eyes.

He smiles at me. "Hey, man!" He steps aside and lets me in.

"Thanks, Jackie. I appreciate the help," I say. I smile at him and pat his shoulder as I enter.

"No problem! Anything to help a friend out!" Jackson says.

Inside, I see two more people. Both my friends. A female and another male. Jasmine. She has long wavy hair with light brown eyes. And then we have Alexander. He's shorter than me but taller than Jasmine. His hair is a bird's nest, always messy. His eyes are dark green, like emeralds.

Jasmine stands up and hugs me tightly. "I'm so sorry for what happened between you and Lily!"

I smile and hug her back. "It's alright. It turns out she was cheating on me for a week or three."

"I've never really liked her," Alexander says. "She sounded awful from the start."

Jackson pats my shoulder. "Hey, man. We're here for you."

I smile. I hear movements on the couch. Alexander got up. He smiles at me. Jasmine still doesn't want to let go of me.

I chuckle. "There is someone I might be interested in."

Finally, Jamsine lets go and looks at me in surprise. "Repeat that!"

"There is someone I might be interested in," I repeat.

"Bro! You just got out of a relationship, and Cupid finds you another love!" Alexander shouts.

We laugh as we think about it. We all sit on the couch and talk about it.

"Who's the lucky girl?" Jasmine asks me.

I slightly blush in embarrassment. I lower my gaze and intertwine my fingers. "Not a woman," I mumble.

We stay silent for a while. Jackson hits my arm. "No way!"

I chuckle and nod.

"What?" Alexander asks.

"Someone's going gay!" Jackson shouts.

I blush more intensely. "Oh, shut up!"

Jasmine and Alexander shake me up. "Tell us! Who's the lucky guy?"

I look at Jackson. He laughs at me as I get shaken up.

"Jackson, I gave him your address. He'll be here soon," I tell him.

We didn't need to wait long. Before we knew it, there was a knock on the door. I stand up and walk toward it. I take a deep breath before opening it.

Peter is standing there with a big smile. "Hey, John!"

I widely smile as I see him. "Hey, Peter! How was your day?"

"My day was alright. There was a lost girl. We safely returned her to her parents," he tells me. "It was weird too. I felt like someone was watching us the whole time."

I swallow hard. "O-oh? Did you see someone?"

He shakes his head. "Not really. The girl did see someone in an alley. I think it was him."

I nod. "Your job must be scary."

He chuckles. "That's why there are brave people who are needed. Not all heroes wear capes!"

I smile at him. He's such a good guy. Kind, brave, and handsome. I can't believe what I'm thinking. Am I really going gay for this man?

He picks up a bag, my bag. "Here are your supplies."

He widely smiles at me as he passes me the bag. I smile back. "Thank you!"

"Anytime," he tells me. "If you ever need someone to talk to, I'm all ears."

His words do something to me. My body does something I didn't know I would ever be able to do. Quickly, I drop the bag and hug him tightly. I feel his arms wrap around me. I shut my eyes and let myself melt in his embrace. He doesn't let go or say a thing. We stay quiet and hug.

After a solid three minutes of hugging, I quickly let go. Wipe away a tear that was rolling down my cheek. "I'm sorry. I don't know what came over me."

I lower my gaze, embarrassed of what I did. I hear a soft chuckle and look at Peter. He smiles. "John, everything is okay. You don't have to apologize for that."

I smile slightly and let the sleeves of my hoodie slide onto my hands. "Still, sorry. It was unexpected."

I look behind me at my friends. They look at me with concern in their gaze. I look back at Peter. He still smiles. I awkwardly smile back. We laugh as it gets too awkward.

Peter looks over my shoulder. I step aside so he can see better. I point as I say their names. "That's Jackson,"

"Wassup!" he says.

"That's Jasmine."

"Hello, dear!" she says.

"And that's Alexander!"

"Hey, mate!" he says.

Peter waves and says: "Hey, guys! Nice meeting you all! I'm Peter!"

I chuckle awkwardly. Peter looks at me as I stand back in front of him.

"A-are you coming in, or do you need to be somewhere?" I ask him.

He shakes his head. "Sorry, I have a meeting in a couple of minutes."

I nod, a bit disappointed. "Alright, good luck with that."

"See you tomorrow?" Peter asks me. "At the café?"

I nod. "Yes, tomorrow at the café."

He smiles again. He looks over my shoulder at my friends and waves. "Take care of him!"

Peter turns back to me and spreads his arms. "Another hug?"

I smile and hug him again. "See you tomorrow, Peter."

"See you tomorrow, John."

We pull away. Peter puts on his police hat and nods goodbye. I nod in response as he leaves.

CHAPTER 3

I take my bag and turn to my friends. They stare at me with different looks. Jasmine looks at me as if I just kissed Peter, Jackson looks a bit more concerned, and Alexander looks between the two.

I smile, slightly embarrassed about what just happened. I shut the door and walk over to the couch. "Alright, ask away!"

"Who's that boy?" Jasmine asks excitedly.

I chuckle. "That was Peter Quintin. He's a cop, and we met at a café."

I see Jackson nod. "And how do you feel?"

"About him or just now?" I ask him.

"Both."

I think for a moment as I open my bag. "I'm alright," I say. "I think I'm in love with him."

I smile as I get out a black notebook.

"That was a long awkward hug," Alexander says. "Are you sure you're okay?"

I nod and open the notebook. "I'm okay."

Write down any problem or thought. This book is for you, and if you allow me, I will read it. - Peter

I widely smile at the note. God, I'm in love with him. I close the book and look at the plain black cover. I may be weird doing this, but I like smelling books. I bring the book to my nose and sniff it.

"I don't remember you having a notebook," Jasmine says. "Did Peter give you that?"

"Yes, he left it in the bag for me," I reply.

Jackson sits next to me. "So, you met him in a café?"

I nod in response.

"And you'll be seeing him back tomorrow?" he asks.

I nod again in response.

"He told you that he felt followed," Jackson says. "Did you...follow him?"

I stop what I'm doing and put the notebook on my lap. "No, I did not. I hope it doesn't happen again."

Jackson nods. Jasmine sits down on the other side, and Alexander follows.

"Want to talk about the breakup?" Alexander asks me.

I sigh. "I will have to one day or another. It's a good idea to tell you when it's still fresh."

Jasmine takes my hand and gently squeezes it. "We're here for you, John."

I smile. "I know, Minnie, I know."

I take a deep breath before explaining what happened. Sometimes I need to stop to breathe, and sometimes a tear rolls down my cheek. I lower my gaze. My hands grip my pants. I quietly sob, and tears fall onto my hands.

Jasmine, Jackson, and Alexander hug me as I cry. We all stay quiet. I see tears in their eyes. We all sob together as real friends.

Minutes pass by. It's almost lunchtime. I chuckle as I realize that we've all just been sitting here. Jasmine looks up at me. "Shut up, big baby. You're the one who brought tears to our eyes!"

I start laughing, and they do the same. I sniff and wipe away my tears. "Coffee? Anyone?" I ask.

They start laughing. "You're the only one here who likes coffee and tea!"

I laugh with them. Jackson jumps off the couch and grabs the phone. "Pizza time!"

We all cheer. "Whoo! Pizza!"

"Order me some coffee too!" I say.

"Don't get any pineapple!" Jasmine shouts.

Jackson hits his chest as if he was offended. "Why would I put a curse on a pizza?"

We start laughing again.

"Don't forget extra peppers for me!" Alexander says.

Jackson winks at him. He starts dialing the number. I get up and walk to the stack of movies in the corner, and Jasmine follows. Alexander goes to the cabinets in the kitchen to get plates.

Alexander puts the plates on the table, and I put the movie in the DVD player. Jackson and Jasmine got more pillows and blankets.

We all sit comfortably on the couch and watch the movie as we wait for the pizza.

There is a knock on the door. "I'll get it!" I say. I jump up from the couch and open the door. I take the food and pay the delivery guy.

As I shut the door, I shouted: "Food's here!"

They throw their arms in the air as I place the food on the table. I give Jackson his pepperoni pizza, Jasmine her fungi, and Alexander his paprika. I give them their drinks and sit back on the couch.

We eat together, watch the movie together, and clean up together. Friends stick together! I'm lucky to have great friends like them. Gosh, I love them!

Jackson helps me inflate the air bed. It may sound like nothing, but it's comfortable.

As the night falls and the moon comes to say hello, Jasmine and Alexander take their leave. I got pillows and blankets from the couch to make it more comfortable.

Jackson and I talk a bit more before bedtime. Around eleven, we head to bed. I try to empty my mind of what happened today and yesterday. I don't want to remember a thing.

I close my eyes and fall asleep not long after. I drift off to a dreamland.

Images flash before my eyes. I see Lily shouting at me. She turns to the guy next to her and kisses him hard. As I look to my left, I see Peter. He smiles at me.

"It's alright, John," he says. "You don't need to worry about a thing."

I step back but trip. I don't hit the ground. I fall and fall and fall. I keep falling into a bottomless black pit. I try to scream, I open my mouth, but no sound comes out.

Finally, I hit the ground. Pain in my back, all the way to my head. I get up and take a look around. Peter stands next to me. I remember this.

This time, I call out his name. He looks at me but doesn't answer. He looks straight through me. His eyes are bloodshot red. His glare burns my skin.

"Betrayer!" "Monster!" "Stalker!" "Criminal!" "Thief!" "Worthless!" "Mistake!" "Disappointment!"

I cover my ears as the words run through my head. I look at Peter. He's not there anymore.

"Peter!" I call out his name.

I feel something in my back, a sudden pain. Something leaves my body. I cough and fall to my knees. I look down and see my shirt soaking in blood. The pain strikes again. It's getting harder and harder to breathe.

It feels like suffocating. I grasp to my stomach where the pain is forming. Blood keeps flowing out. I look up and see Peter.

"H-help..." I hoarsely say.

The words are barely said. I feel blood leaving the corner of my lips. Peter holds a knife to my throat. The blade is bloody. He lifts my chin with a sly grin. "Goodbye."

He lifts the knife and attacks.

CHAPTER 4

I get woken up by Jackson. He shakes me up with a concerned look. I sit up in shock. My pajama is soaking in sweat. My head turns as I rub my eyes.

I look at Jackson. My breathing is heavy.

"John? Are you alright?" Jack asks me.

I shake my head and bring my knees to my chest. "I had a nightmare, a horrible nightmare..."

"Want to talk about it?" Jackson asks. "You were screaming in your sleep, trembling from top to toe."

"I saw Lily break up with me again. She kissed that guy," I say. I look down. "Peter was there too. I stepped back and fell."

I swallow hard as I remember the pain. "I couldn't scream. Nothing came out. I finally hit the ground. Bad words filled my mind. I was in a dark alley. Peter was there."

I look at Jackson with pain in my voice. "He stabbed me... He stabbed me..."

Jackson looks at me. He looks worried. "Want me to stay with you for the rest of the night?"

I shake my head. "I won't be getting any more sleep tonight."

I feel him put his hand on my shoulder. "Johny, I'm your friend. I'm staying."

He smiles slightly. A small smile appears on my face. I let myself sink back into a lying position. He lies next to me.

"When you wake up, I'll be there for you. If you have another nightmare, I'll be there," Jackson whispers.

I feel myself falling back to sleep. My eyelids are getting heavier and heavier by the second. I close my eyes and fall asleep. This time, I don't have any dreams I remember.

Days pass by. I haven't been to the café to see Peter or anything. The nightmares lessen every day.

Finally, I dare to go out and see Peter again. I've been ignoring his texts and calls too. I take a deep breath before entering the café.

I do the usual. Order some coffee, take a seat, and wait. I look around the café for Peter. I don't see him. A cashier calls out my name. I stand up, and of course, I have to trip.

I expect to fall face-first, but it never happens. My sweatshirt feels tight around my chest. Someone grabbed my clothes before I could even hit the ground.

Confused, I place my hands on the ground and stand up. I dust off the dust from my hands and turn around.

Peter is standing in front of me with a surprised facial expression.

I try to smile, but it looks as if I just got hit in the teeth. I want to say something, but the words won't leave my mouth.

I turn around and walk at a fast pace to the cashier. He chuckles as he gives me my coffee. I drop my money because of how much my hands tremble.

"Hey, take your time," the cashier says. "Relax and take it easy."

I chuckle nervously. "Easier said than doing it!"

The cashier softly laughs. "I have a sister just like you. Nervous and clumsy."

I smile at him as I give him the money. He nods, and I take my coffee. I turn around and almost bump into Peter.

"AH!" I shout as I see him. "Oh, geez! You scared me!"

He takes my shoulders and shakes me. "And you scared me!"

He points his finger at me. "One week! One week and you didn't even say hi! You didn't come!"

I freeze and fall onto my knees. Peter steps back. "John? Oh, god, John! I'm so sorry!"

He kneels before me and checks if I'm okay. A cashier comes from behind the counter to check on both of us. I place my head on Peter's shoulder. "Don't do that again, please..." I whisper.

I feel him nodding. "I'm sorry."

I stand up again, and so do the cashier and Peter. When Peter gets his coffee, we both go outside.

We walk together to the police station and along the way.

"I had a horrible nightmare and didn't dare to leave the building," I tell him. "It was horrifying."

He smiles at me. "Luckily, your friends took care of you."

I smile back. "Yes, and I'm grateful to have amazing friends like them."

"Oh! I'm so going to tell them that you said that when I see them!" he replies as he bumps into my arm.

I laugh and reply: "Oh, no! I'm going to die from shame!"

We both laugh on our way to the police station. When we arrive, we both fall silent.

He looks at me and says: "Hey... When there's something, call me."

I smile at him and nod. "I will."

Peter lowers his gaze. "Man, I wish we could hang out more often."

I bump his elbow. "We have lunchtime!"

He smiles back but shakes his head. "I need to do fieldwork today."

I look surprised at him with a hint of concern. He chuckles at my reaction and places a hand on my shoulder. "Relax, I'll be fine. I trained for this!"

A man comes to us. He doesn't look like an officer. "Hello, gentlemen. Am I interrupting?"

I look confused at him. Peter and the man laugh.

"John, meet the detective," Peter says.

The man holds out his hand. "Pleasure to meet you. I'm Anderson, Marcus Anderson."

I smile and shake the hand. "John Welling. The pleasure is mine, sir."

He nods and lets go of my hand. He looks at Peter and asks: "Ready?"

Peter nods confidently. Mr. Anderson looks back at me. "Finish your conversation. Again, it was a pleasure."

With that said, he turns around and enters the building. I smile at the ground. Peter bumps my arm. I look at him.

"You're worried, aren't you?" he asks me.

I nod and reply: "Don't die, please."

He smiles. "You already lost someone. You're not going to lose me."

I smile. Peter faces the entrance again and sighs. "See you tomorrow?"

"Tomorrow," I reply.

Peter enters the building, leaving me behind. I want to turn around and walk away, but my body betrays me and makes me do something else. Instead of turning around, I ran inside.

"Wait!" I shout.

Peter and Marcus turn around. I run into Peter and hug him as tightly as possible. He freezes. I hear his breathing stop. I let go of him. I feel people stare at us. I nod once. "Bye, Peter! Good luck!"

I turn around and leave as quickly as possible. What the fuck did I just do? Why did I do that in front of so many officers?

As I turn around the corner, I decrease my pace to a stop. I sit down, exhausted from the run. I chuckle when I realize how Peter reacted. So cute!

CHapTer 5

The day passes by. I go back to Jackson's place and relax on the couch. I told Jackson what happened, and we couldn't stop laughing.

As the night falls, we go to bed. Jackson sleeps back in his room after the nightmares lessened. I shut my eyes and hope that I will be able to see Peter.

In the morning, I wake up, do my morning routine, and quietly leave the house. Jackson isn't awake yet.

I walk to the café while humming with the chirping birds. The smell of freshly baked bread fills the air as I pass by the bakery, the smell of meat and seasoning fills the air around the butchery, and the smell of coffee fills the air around the café.

I enter the café with a wide smile. I get my coffee and look for a seat. As I walk toward the table, I feel a tap on my shoulder. I turn around and see Marcus with Peter.

Again, I smile at both. "Good morning, officers!"

"Good morning, John!" Peter says. I can see him lower his gaze for some reason. I think he's blushing. "That was very unexpected yesterday."

The blushing isn't from love. He feels awkward. I nod as I remember. I feel my cheeks get slightly red. "Y-yeah! Yesterday!"

I hear Mr. Anderson chuckle. I look at him, and he shakes his head. "You two are unbelievable!"

I sigh from the embarrassing feelings inside me. I forgot Marcus was next to Peter when I hugged him.

Peter clears his throat. "How about I get coffee while you two find a seat? Good plan? Good plan."

Without waiting for our answer, Peter goes to a cashier and orders coffee. Anderson gestures to a table. I nod with a smile and walk toward it. We both sit down and chat a bit before Peter returns.

"So, John. How did you two meet?" Mr. Anderson asks.

I smile as I place my coffee on the table and cross my arms before replying: "We met at this café. I tripped. Peter caught me before I hit the floor."

Marcus laughs softly. "Amazing story, pal."

I nod and smile. Marcus squints his eyes as he looks at me. He stares at me as I sit there. As I start feeling uncomfortable, I lower my gaze but still feel his upon me.

I take my coffee and look at it under the table. I don't drink yet. Confused, I notice my hands trembling.

"So, you're a detective?" I ask Marcus.

"Yes, I am. I sense that you're afraid," Marcus replies. "You can relax. No one's watching."

I crush the cup, causing burning hot coffee to spill over my lap. In reflex, I stand up in shock. Marcus gets some tissues for me and helps me. Peter comes over quickly with a bottle of water.

The coffee burns as I feel it on my skin. Peter pours cold water over my legs.

It takes a while for me to feel comfortable. When I feel better, I sit back down. I apologize to the people around us for the sudden movements.

Everything goes back to normal. I sigh. I've done something stupid again.

Peter sits down. "Are you alright? What happened?"

I open my mouth to answer, but Marcus beats me to it. "He felt tense, so I tried calming him down. I think I made it worse because he crushed his coffee cup."

Shutting my mouth, I look back down. My hands are on my lap, and they're still trembling. It could be from the coffee, but it could also be from fear.

Why did Marcus tell me that no one was watching?

I clear my throat and excuse myself. I stand up and leave the building at a fast pace. Now, I can think of nothing more but the following. I didn't mean to stalk Peter.

I hear Peter call after me as I turn around the corner. I start running.

"Run faster! They're going to get you!" a voice tells me.

No one around me talked to me.

"RUN!"

I panic and continue to run. Faster and faster, no looking back.

"RUN, RUN, RUN!"

"SHUT UP!" I shout.

I cover my ears.

In the middle of a road, I trip over my shoelaces. I see a car coming right at me.

Someone pulls me back onto the sidewalk before the car hits me. My heart skips a beat, maybe more than one. Adrenaline kicks in as I see the car pass by before my eyes. My breathing pattern has changed.

I let myself lie on the ground to catch my breath. My chest goes up and down with every breath that I take.

Someone has pulled me back onto the sidewalk. I try to get back onto my feet but am stopped and pulled back down by the man who saved me. I struggle as I try to break free.

That man grabs my shoulders and pins me to the ground. He mounts over me to make me see his face. "John! Calm down!"

I see Marcus's face. He saved me. My breathing doesn't go back to its natural pattern. I cough as I gasp for air. Marcus lets me go, and I immediately lie down on my side and roll into a ball.

Every breath sounds hoarse. I calm down as my breathing goes back to normal. I don't want to experience that again.

It felt like an anvil dropping onto my lungs. My throat feels dry, and I cough again. I roll onto my back and see Peter bending over me. I chuckle. "Hey..."

My voice is hoarse. I can still smile and laugh. I sit up and sigh. "Does anyone happen to have a bottle of water?"

Peter kneels beside me and passes me a bottle. I smile as I thank him. As I unscrew the cap, Marcus asks me: "What was that back there?"

I shrug and finish the bottle of water in seconds. "I don't know. That was unexpected, even for me."

Peter places a hand on my shoulder. "Yesterday, you told me to not die. Who's the one who almost died, now?"

I chuckle. "Relax! I'm still alive!"

"Oh, you bloody bastard!" Peter says. I do see him smile.

Marcus is the only one who seems concerned.

"What?" I ask him. "We can still laugh."

He sighs deeply before replying: "You almost died. How can you laugh?"

Without meaning to, I start to laugh. I can't seem to stop. I laugh and laugh and laugh. "I'm sorry! I'm sorry!"

I see Peter's smile disappear in the corner of my eye. I clear my throat again and lower my gaze. "Sorry, I don't know what came upon me."

Marcus sighs. "Have you been feeling watched or anything?"

Confused, I look at him. "How did you know?"

I don't feel watched, but I play along.

Marcus gestures at Peter. "Peter told me he felt watched. I have a feeling you feel the same."

I nod. "I do feel eyes upon me. I don't leave the house often due to reasons. That's one of them."

Peter gently bumps my arm. I look at him. "Why didn't you tell me when I told you about me?"

I shrug and reply: "I don't know. I guess I did want to be a bother."

Peter and I looked at each other for a long time. He sighs and suddenly pulls me in for a hug.

Oh, his body was burning. The heat was comforting. I bury my face into his chest. He doesn't seem to mind it. He wears perfume. Peter wears perfume! It smells like oak wood with a hint of lavender.

My heart starts to beat faster as I relax in his embrace. I don't know why. I want more.

I pull away. Peter seems surprised by my actions.

"I-I'm sorry," I say. "You must think I'm this kind of a freak or something."

"Hey, look at me," Peter says.

I look him in the eyes. I realize a tear has rolled down my face.

"You are not a freak. You, John, are amazing! No matter what people tell you, you are a good friend."

I scoff as more tears roll down my face. I wipe them away. "Thank you, Peter. Thank you."

I see him smile. I look at Marcus. He chuckles. "When you're ready, you can come with us, or go to a friend. It would be better to have a friend by your side."

With a smile, I agree. "I'll be going to my friend's place," I say. I look at Peter. "You know the address."

Peter nods.

I nod in reply and stand up. Peter and Marcus stand up too. I stretch out.

Peter laughs. "You should work out more!"

"Hey! Don't blame me for not being an agent!" I reply and laugh.

Marcus shakes his head while chuckling.

"Well, I'll be taking my leave. You two are already late because of me," I say.

Peter pats my back. "It's okay, John. You didn't die!"

We laugh as we see Marcus roll his eyes. He claps his hands. "Alright, are you two done?"

Peter nods. "Yes, we are!"

He looks at me and says: "Just in case you wanted to hang out. I'll be going to a small bar later. Call me if you want any details."

I nod and thank him.

Marcus and Peter go to their work while I go back to Jackson's place. When I stand at the door, I hesitate to open the door.

"Fuck..." I mumble to myself.

I sigh and turn around. I have a problem. I walk toward the police station. I wait on the other side of the street and stand in a dark alley.

Hours pass by. Jackson has called me six times. I look at the time. It's five o'clock in the afternoon. Finally, I see Peter leave the building.

He walks away, and I follow.

CHaPTer 6

Peter walks at a fast pace. I follow him from across the street. He enters a building. It must be the bar he was telling me about.

I cross the street and enter the same building. As I enter, the smell of alcohol fills my nose. I look around. There are small tables in the center and larger tables by the walls.

At the counter, I see multiple girls trying to hit on the two bartenders. I looked around to find Peter. He's sitting down at the counter. I walk to a table in a darker corner.

People play darts in another corner. Some people are already drunk. I see Peter order something that looks like whisky. I didn't expect him to drink something like that.

I see a man walk over to him. I keep an eye on them. They both seem to talk ordinarily. Twenty minutes later, Peter and the guy already drunk a couple of drinks. I sense that that's the meaning of the guy. He still looks alright.

I see him flirt with Peter. I feel anger and jealousy boil inside me. The man strokes Peter's thighs. Peter shakes his hand and stands up. He puts money on the counter and leaves the bar.

I stay inside and look at the man. The man stands up and leaves the bar. Angrily, I follow him. I see him follow Peter. I follow right behind them.

In an alley, I find a pipe. I take it and keep it with me. I hear footsteps behind me.

"Who are you?" I hear a male voice ask.

I don't turn around yet. "I'm no one."

I hear him come closer. He puts a hand on my shoulder and turns me around.

Keeping the pipe tightly in my grip, I hit the man as I turned. "Stay away from him!"

The man coughs as he is down on his knees. I see blood dripping onto the ground.

"ASSHOLE!" the man yells.

I chuckle. "Me? An asshole? You're the big motherfucker who tries to hook up with strangers."

The man stands up and tries to grab my face. I need to step aside to avoid him. I scoff. "So easy..."

With the pipe, I hit his head again. He falls onto the ground and tries to get up. I place my foot on his chest. "Peter is mine. I don't want to share."

I point the pipe at him.

"P-please!" the man begs.

"Please? Oh, please! Dear god, save my soul!" I laugh as I mock him.

I step off him and grip the pipe tighter.

"STAY!"

I hit him.

"AWAY!"

I hit him.

"FROM PETER!"

I hit him again.

I keep hitting and hitting and hitting him. His head burst open, I hear his bones break, and see blood splatter onto the ground. I keep hitting him with a smile.

Smiling widely, I step back and throw away the pipe. Adrenaline pumps in my blood as I pant. I chuckle. I laugh. I take my time to look at my masterpiece.

Blood spreads around the body. His head is open. His skin turns pale from the amount of blood loss.

I turn around and walk out of the alley. The evidence is right there. I'm wearing gloves.

There's blood on my shirt. I take my jacket and cover my shirt with it. I happily hum as I walk back to Jackson's place.

"John!" I hear a familiar voice say. I turn around to see who it is. I force a smile as I see Marcus Anderson.

"Marcus! Such a surprise. What are you doing here late at night?" I ask.

He doesn't seem that happy. "Are you alright?"

I nod.

"Have you heard any screaming?" he asks.

I act confused and shake my head. "No, sorry," I pause. "Is there something you want to tell me?"

"Someone was murdered."

I freeze. I realize what I've done. Of course, the police would find out. I left the weapon and the body there. Luckily, there were no witnesses.

My breathing stops. Marcus places a hand on my shoulder. "Relax, I'm here with you." He takes a good look at me. "Do you feel nauseous?"

I nod.

"It's alright. Sit down if you need to," Marcus says. "The police will come over any minute. Do you want me to call someone for you?"

I sink onto my knees. My legs are jelly. Marcus kneels next to me and checks if I'm hot.

"Marcus! John!" I look to my right and see Peter running toward us. "Hey!"

Sirens. I hear sirens. The police are coming.

"Peter? You look pale. Are you okay?" Marcus asks.

"Someone made me drunk. Luckily I sober up quickly," Peter replies. He looks at me. "Now tell me what is going on?"

"Murder...dead..." I mumble. "Someone's dead."

I swallow my other words. A sick feeling fills my stomach. I grasp the painful spot. Peter tugs my jacket and turns me to him. "Let me take this off you."

He opens the jacket, stops, and stares. His breathing stopped. I look down at my bloody shirt. Police run over to us.

Blood is on my shirt and my hands. I cough, bend over, and throw up in disgust. Peter and Marcus step back. I cough and cough.

"I want to go home..." I mumble. "P-please..."

Peter helps me up. "We'll see what we can do, buddy. Stay with us."

Marcus and Peter put me on a bench. Another officer puts a blanket around me. I keep it close. Someone comes over to us with a first aid kit. They check me.

They don't find a wound. The officer gives me a suspicious look. I have a choice. I can choose between lying or the truth. I shut my eyes and look down.

I lean against Peter, who sits beside me. I can feel his concerned look on me.

"Will he come back?" I ask. "Will that guy come back?"

The three look confused at me.

"What do you mean?" Peter asks me.

I show my forearm. There is a massive bruise on it. I'm kind of lucky that I fell down the stairs.

They all look at it in shock.

"Will he come back?" I ask again.

I act afraid. I'm lying. I will end up in jail for this.

"Murder!"

I look around after I flinch. My breathing quickens.

I cover my ears.

"I'm not insane! I'm not insane! I'm not insane! I'm not insane!" I repeat the words over and over again.

In the corner of my eye, I see Peter scared.

"Someone's here! I hear him!" I shout.

I tremble and breathe quicker and quicker. Marcus and Peter try to calm me down.

Peter kneels in front of me. I look him in the eyes. "Everything is okay. You're safe with us. No one's here."

I cover my ears and put my head on my lap. "I'm so tired..."

I feel a hand on my back. "May we use your phone?" Marcus asks me.

I nod.

Peter searches my pockets for my phone. When he finds it, I unlock it. He goes to my contacts and calls the latest person who called me. Jackson.

After the second ring, he picks up.

"John! Where have you been? Why haven't you called back?" I hear Jackson ask. He sounds mad.

"Hey, Jackson! Sorry, I'm Peter, the cop who once came to your place for John," Peter replies.

"Peter? What's going on? Where's John?" Jackson asks in reply. There's a sudden tone of concern in his voice.

"Could you come to the candy shop 'Lollies and More' next to the flower shop?" Peter asks. "John is with us. We'll explain everything later."

Jackson falls silent. "Are those sirens I hear in the background?"

"Sadly, yes."

"Jackie? C-could you please just come?" I hoarsely ask.

"Oh, Jesus Christ! You sound horrible! Stay where you are! I'm coming!" Jackson replies.

Jackson hangs up. He's such a good friend.

I look to my left and see a body bag lifted into a car. Peter and Marcus follow my gaze. Peter looks at Marcus and asks: "Could you stay with John? I want to look at the body."

Marcus nods in reply. Peter looks at me and taps my thigh for my attention. I look at him, and he smiles slightly. "I'll be right back, okay?"

I nod. Peter stands up and walks toward the body. I watch him walk away. The body gets put on the ground, and the bag gets opened. I see a glimpse of the burst-open head.

Marcus turns my head toward the ground. "You shouldn't have seen that."

My body trembles in fear. I cover my face with my hands. I feel sick and nauseous. I'm disgusted by myself.

"John? How do you feel?" Marcus asks.

"Sick. I am d-disgusted," I reply, my voice still hoarse.

Marcus sighs. "That's normal, boy. It is."

The officer with the med kit hands me a bag. I take the bag and open it just in case I would need to throw up.

I hear a car on my right side. Two officers go over there. The officers argue with a female and two males. The officers stand in front of the people. I can't see who it is.

I sigh and look at Peter. I see the body. I look back down at the bag and vomit.

Damnit! Why did I have to look? I cough and spit out any leftovers. Marcus pats my back. I hear someone running toward us.

"John!" a voice shouts. It's Jackson.

Jackson kneels in front of me. Alexander stands beside him while he keeps Jasmine close. Jasmine has tears in her eyes.

I smile. "Y-you came..." I cough.

"Fuck, man... What happened to you?" Jackson asks me. He feels my forehead for heat.

"Murder," Marcus answers for me. "Someone has died. He was involved."

Everyone falls silent.

"I know that guy," someone says. Peter is back. I wave at him. He smiles and nods. "How are you feeling?"

I shrug. "I'm tired."

I pull the blanket tight around me as a sudden cold hits me. It sends shivers down my spine. My eyelids start feeling heavy. I'm so tired.

Peter sits back down next to me and lets me lean against him. He puts an arm around me.

"You can sleep, John. We can talk about this another day," Peter tells me. "It's okay."

I feel my eyes close. My body feels weak. I fell asleep after some time.

CHaPTer 7

I open my eyes. The light is bright, and I squint my eyes. I take a deep breath before sitting up.

I take a look around me. It's Jackson's place. They must've brought me here when I was unconscious. I rub my eyes before calling out his name. I hear multiple noises coming from the bedroom. Jackson storms into the room, his shirt covered in yogurt.

"John! How do you feel?" he asks me. He kneels beside the mattress. "Tell me, buddy."

I chuckle as I look at him from top to toe. "I'm alright. A bit light-headed, but alright. What about you? What happened?"

Jackson sighs, relieved. "Bro, I was just happy to be hearing your voice. I was worried, man."

Jasmine runs out of Jackson's room and trips. Alexander follows and trips over Jasmine's legs. I can't help but laugh. I see them pant and smile in relief.

I cross my legs and cross my arms. "Will someone tell me what's going on?" I ask.

Jackson looks confused at me. "You don't remember what happened yesterday?"

I shake my head. "Sorry, man. I don't remember anything."

I feel a slight pain in my forearm and look at it. I pull up my sleeve and see the big bruise on my arm. "How did that get there?"

I chuckle and look at them all. "Very funny. Who did this?"

As I look at Jasmine and Alexander, they lower their gaze. My smile fades, and I look at Jackson. He shakes his head.

"Who did this?" I ask again. "This isn't funny anymore."

"John..." I look to my right. Jackson presses his lips together.

"Someone attacked you," Jasmine says. "Someone was murdered yesterday. The cops found you with your shirt and hands covered in blood."

Now I remember. I killed someone. I look down at my hands. I feel like a damn monster.

Jackson pats my shoulder. "It's still morning. Perhaps Peter is in the café."

He smiles as he tries to make me feel better. I smile back and nod. I stand up and walk toward my bag with clothes. I take out a black hoodie and some sports pants. I look at the others.

"How the fuck do you survive in that? It's bloody summer! " Alexander says.

I laugh. "I like the heat."

It's just cold for me.

I turn and walk toward the bathroom, where I put on my clothes. I shrug as I look in the mirror. A couple of bruises here and there, nothing to worry about.

I put the hood on and put on sunglasses. I walk out of the bathroom and act like a buff guy. "So! Mission to the café!" I shout.

They all burst out in laughter. I stay in my act and say: "Oh, ho, ho! Laughter? Someone wants to get kicked in the ass!"

Jackson falls over and hits the ground with his hand as he laughs. Jasmine leans against the couch as she tries not to fall over. Alexander fell onto the floor with tears. I start laughing too.

I take off the hood and sunglasses. I shake my head as I try to stop laughing. Walking toward the door, I look at the three, still dying of laughter.

"Alright, alright!" I shout and put my hands in the air. "I'm going to the café. Anyone who wants to come?"

After a few seconds, they calmed down. Jasmine and Alexander raise their hands. "We want to come!" they shout.

The three of us look at Jackson. He rolls his eyes and sighs. "Fine! Only because you three are going!"

Jackson stands up and gets a new shirt.

I open the door and act like a gentleman. "After you!"

They laugh, and we leave the house.

Together, we walk to the café. When we arrived, I stopped in front of the entrance. I look through the windows to see any glimpses of Peter. I don't see him.

My friends sense my nervousness.

"Hey," Jasmine says. "Everything will be alright."

She holds out her hand to me with a smile. I smile back and take her hand. Together, we enter the building.

We go to the counter and order our coffees. We look around to find a table. I look around for Peter. Alexander points to a table. Jackson grabs my arm and pulls me with him.

I trip over my shoelaces and fall onto the ground.

"Oh, shit! I'm so sorry!" Jackson shouts. He kneels beside me and helps me up.

As I get back on my feet, I realize how much pain my body is in. I grasp my right forearm with the bruise. It stings.

"John!" a voice shouts. I turn around and see Peter.

I take a look at him from top to toe. He wears tight black jeans with a blue shirt. His collar is a bit open.

My jaw drops to the ground as I try to form words.

Peter cocks his head to one side in confusion. He looks so hot. Why am I thinking this? I shouldn't think about this!

I turn around. Alexander can't hide his smirk. Jasmine raises an eyebrow with a suspicious smile.

"What am I supposed to do?" I mouth them.

Jackson snorts and does what I never wanted him to do. "Hey, Peter! You're looking fine today!"

My heart stops. I force a smile and turn around. I wave awkwardly. "H-hey! How's everything going?"

I shut my eyes and press my lips shut. I raise my shoulders in shame.

I hear a soft chuckle. I open my eyes and see Peter smile. "Thanks for the compliment, you two." His smile fades. "I'm doing alright, but I should be asking you."

I sigh and scratch my neck. Crossing my arms, I reply: "Yeah, I'm doing alright! I have a couple of bruises. Don't worry about it."

Biting my lip, I lower my head with a bit of shame. I shouldn't have said that. With a tap on my shoulder, I look up. Peter looks concerned into my eyes. His glare digs deep into mine.

"Sit down."

Peter gestures to the free table against the wall. I do as told and walk toward the table with my head held low. As I sit down, the rest follow. Peter sits next to me.

Taking a deep breath, I look at him. He smiles. "I want to talk about business, John. Is that okay with you? Want to wait?"

I shake my head. "I'm ready."

Peter looks at the others. They nod. Peter's smile fades and turns into a more serious expression.

"The murder has begun a case, my case," Peter starts. "Am I allowed to ask questions?"

Peter looks at me with a questioning look. I nod in reply. I see a slight smile tug at the corner of his lips. He takes out a small notebook.

"Did you see any faces except the murdered guy?" Peter asks me.

I shake my head. "I didn't see his face. He did have a male voice."

Peter writes it down in the small notebook. "Can you describe his voice?"

I frown as I try to find an answer. I end up shaking my head again. "I can't remember, sorry."

"That's alright." Peter scribbles in his notebook again. "How did you get the bruises?"

"Pipe. He had great force. He hit me in the stomach, arms, and legs," I answer.

Without thinking, I start scratching the bruise on my forearm.

Peter writes another thing in his notebook. He doesn't seem to notice.

My heart skips a beat when I hear my name. Our coffee is ready. I look up at my friends. "I'll get it," Alexander says. He stands up and gets our coffee.

I look at Peter. Peter looks serious. His hair falls majestic over his forehead. My heart races just watching him. Without thinking, my eyes fall onto his collar that's open. His collarbone is visible.

I look back at his face. He's frowning and has his pen by his lips. God, what do I want to bite that lip.

Peter looks at me, and I look down at my lap in reaction. I hear a soft chuckle. I look back at Peter's face. He smiles at me. "Sorry, I get lost in my thoughts," he says. "Did you need anything?"

I shake my head. "It's nothing. Sorry, I stared."

Alexander sits back down with our drinks. He places our coffee on the table.

I make a painful expression as a sudden pain hits my arm. Peter looks worried and examines my whole body. He takes my forearm and puts it on the table. It's bleeding.

"Did you scratch your arm?" Peter asks me. He takes some tissues and gently daps off the blood.

I press my lips together and nod. "I guess I was nervous."

"You don't need to be nervous, buddy. It's alright," Peter comforts me. "But it's normal."

He smiles slightly. Peter looks at the others. "Could someone please get a Band-Aid?"

The three stand up all at once. This awkward moment lasts for a second or two. The three end up going to the cashier together. Peter and I are left alone at the table.

Peter's movements are so gentle. He presses the tissue against my arm so carefully. "This will have to do until they come back," he tells me. He looks back at my face and smiles confidently.

"How do you feel?" Peter asks.

I smile slightly and answer: "I'm fine. A bit ashamed of myself, but fine."

"There's nothing to be ashamed of, John," Peter reassures me. "It's not the first time someone hurt himself due to nervousness."

My smile widens at his words. Jasmine puts a first aid kit on the table. The others sit back down. Peter takes the first aid kit and opens it. He searches for cotton balls, Band-aids, and an antiseptic.

When he finds them, he unscrews the cap of the antiseptic. My smile fades as I realize this will hurt.

Peter pours the liquid onto a cotton ball and gently takes my arm. I pull it away.

I can hear Alexander snort. With my lips pressed tightly together, I shake my head. Peter squints his eyes and tries to take my arm. I pull away again and shake my head.

I can hear Peter inhale sharply. "John, I need to put antiseptic on it," he says. "Please, give me your arm."

I shake my head again. "No, thank you!"

Jasmine starts to giggle while Alexander and Jackson burst out in laughter. Peter turns to them. "What?" he asks.

"Let's just say that John has a terrible experience with antiseptic!" Alexander says, half laughing.

Jasmine tries to breathe when she says: "Last time, he poured half a bottle on accident on a big wound, and he screamed like a little girl!"

I look down as I remember that moment. It burned like a fucking Hell!

Peter chuckles and looks back at me. "John, how do you even do that?" Peter asks me.

I shrug as I don't know the answer. "I'm very clumsy!" I say in defense.

Peter holds up the antiseptic-covered cotton ball. "Look, this will only hurt a bit. Please, give me your arm."

I shake my head again. "No!"

Peter sighs with a soft chuckle. "Geez, you're like a child."

Jackson stands up and grabs my arm. Jasmine stands on the other side and takes my other arm, just in case I do something wild. Jackson holds out my arm toward Peter.

Peter shrugs and gently presses the wound with the antiseptic-covered cotton ball. It stings! I do my best to pull away my arm with no luck.

Peter quickly finishes it by putting on a Band-Aid.

Jackson and Jasmine released me. I lean with my back against the wall with my legs on my chair. I look at Peter with a devil's stare.

"Okay, John, relax. It was necessary," Jackson says.

I hiss at him. Everyone falls quiet.

"Okay..." Alexander breaks the silence. "John turned into a beast."

Peter chuckles nervously. "Come on, now. It was necessary."

I stick out my tongue and put on my hood while I grab my coffee. I take a sip while I still look Peter dead in the eye. I can sense his uneasiness.

I start coughing as I forget to blow before drinking. "Damn hot coffee!"

Everyone starts to laugh. I can't help but laugh too.

"This is the second time you forgot!" Peter laughs.

I feel my cheeks flush in embarrassment. Why does this always happen to me?

After a minute or ten, Peter takes out his notebook again. "Are you ready for more questions?" he asks us.

I nod, and so does the rest.

"Alright. What was your relationship with the murdered man?" Peter asks.

"I've never seen that man before," I answer. "This was the first time."

Peter writes that down and asks the next question. "Why did you act so normal on the streets?"

I frown. "What do you mean?"

Peter clicks the pen once before asking: "Mr. Anderson told me he found you humming happily on the streets."

I swallow as the guilt eats me alive. I lower my gaze and feel my hands go toward my bruises again.

"I was forced to act normal. The killer said nothing would happen. He held a knife to my throat," I lie. "The man was killed before my eyes. I don't know why he spared me."

I swallow again. Peter places his hand on top of mine. I was squeezing my arm. I loosen my grip and look at the left marks.

"Sorry," I say. "I don't know what came over me."

I hear Peter sigh. "Want to continue this another time?"

I nod in reply. "Perhaps that's a good idea."

I take my cup and realize that I'm trembling. Peter puts his hand on the cap and places the cup back on the table. "Relax. Take a deep breath."

I do as told and take a deep breath.

"How about we go outside?" Peter asks.

I nod. Peter stands up and holds out his hand. I take it and stand up. He smiles at me. I want to do so many things to him.

The five of us take our coffee and step outside.

I take a deep breath as we are outside. It feels as if I could sink onto the ground at any moment.

We walk around a bit as everything gets better. We joke and laugh as we try to forget about earlier.

"What's the biggest clumsiness thing you've done?" Peter asks me.

I inhale sharply as the rest laugh. "Okay, this one was from about a year ago," I say. "Jackson and I were walking to the skate park."

"This one is funny!" Jackson shouts.

"Wait! The skate park? Peter asks.

Jasmine chuckles. "John! You've never told him you can skate?"

I shake my head. "Nope! Never!"

Peter bumps my arm. "John!"

I laugh and continue. "Anyways! We were walking toward the skate park. Then in the middle of the street, I trip."

Peter already laughs.

"And I was like: 'Oh, shit!'. I fell face-first. The cars stopped as fast as possible. You could hear the tires screech!"

The rest start to laugh too.

"So, there was this whole accident just because I tripped!"

Peter slams his hand against my shoulder out of laughter and asks me: "How can you be so clumsy?"

I shrug. "My mother always said I could be whatever I want. I became a problem!"

A couple of days have passed. They're still looking for the murderer, me. They don't have a suspicion. I answered all the questions Peter asked.

I can't seem to get him out of my mind. Those lips, that collarbone, that scent, and those deep eyes are stuck in my head.

I want to bite those lips, I want to kiss that collarbone, I want that smell all over me, and I want those eyes to look deep into mine. I want everything.

Lately, I've been following him more often. I can't seem to stop. I watch his every move. I watch him eat, drink, and do his job. Sometimes I would even go over to his house.

Peter. Is. Mine.

CHAPTER 8

One day, I go to the café and wait for Peter. My phone rings, and I take it out.

"Hello?" I answer the call.

"Hey, John," I hear Peter say. "Sorry, I'm not feeling well."

"Oh, are you alright? Do you have a cold?" I ask.

I hear Peter cough. "One moment, please."

Peter clears his throat before saying: "I'm a bit sick. I won't be leaving the house any time soon."

"Do you need anything? Would you like me to do something for you?" I ask.

"That's very kind of you, John. I don't need anything now," Peter replies. "I just know that you wait for me every day. It'll be hot today. I don't want you to melt."

I chuckle at his comment. "Melting in the sun like ice? That would never happen!"

I hear him chuckle.

"You should rest, Peter. I'll call Marcus for you," I say with a small smile.

"Thank you, mate," Peter says. "You're a great friend."

We hang up. I smile and dial Marcus's number.

He picks up after the third ring. "With Marcus Anderson."

"Hey, Marcus. It's me, John," I answer.

"Oh, hello, John. Why did you call?" he asks me.

"Peter won't be coming to work for a couple of days. He's not feeling well," I tell him.

"Ah, that's alright. Thank you for telling me," Marcus replies. "Anything else?"

"Not that I know," I reply. "You?"

Marcus seems to be thinking. There's silence on the other side. Finally, he replies: "Nothing much on my side either."

I nod. "Alright. Have a good day further."

"You too, John."

We hang up. I'm left alone on the streets. Instead of getting my daily coffee, I walk further. I walk toward Peter's house.

When I see his house, I turn and go to his backyard. The only thing that separates the path and his yard is a fence. Luckily, it's not that high, and I can climb it.

His yard is big. He has multiple flowers and plants and one big sloping tree. I've done this before, climbing in his tree.

When I arrive at his fence, I look around for people. No one's there. I climb into the yard. Peter isn't watching. I look at the big tree. With care, I climb into it. I use the leaves as a cover.

I see Peter in his bed. He stands up and stretches as he yawns. He walks downstairs. I watch his every movement. He goes to the kitchen and makes breakfast.

When he's finished, he goes to the hallway. I can't see the hallway. He comes back with a newspaper and sits at the table. He reads while he eats. I stare at him as he does so.

He suddenly raises his head. He turns to the hallway. I have a feeling the doorbell just rang. Peter places his newspaper aside and walks toward the hallway. I watch with care.

He comes back smiling. I squint my eyes as I try to find out why.

He steps aside and lets in a woman. A sudden rage of jealousy hits me. Who is she?

The woman hugs Peter tightly. When they let go, Peter gestures to one of the empty chairs.

Peter goes to the kitchen. I see him take another mug from the cabinet. He pours coffee into it and gives it to the woman. I see him say something before he disappears into the hallway.

He goes to the bathroom. There's a small window where I can see him through. He lifts his shirt, revealing his muscular body. I look away as I feel my cheeks get hot.

Are cops supposed to be this muscular? Why is he built like this? I hesitate to look back.

I take a deep breath as I try to calm down. Finally, I decided to look again.

Goodness, he's so handsome. I kind of regret looking away. He has changed his pants already. I groan as I cover my mouth with my hand. My cheeks flush.

I want him so badly.

Peter turns around. I quickly hide behind more leaves. I see him look out of the window. Peter looks around the yard.

He pulls the curtains. Damn it.

After a couple of minutes, I see him back at the dining table. He sits with the woman. I get jealous again.

I watched them for fifteen minutes.

I can't help but break a stick as I see the woman blush slightly. I have had enough of this. I turn around and jump right over the fence. I walk toward the street in front of Peter's house.

Hiding behind cars, I watch them. After a couple of minutes, the woman finally leaves the house. Peter waves goodbye before getting back inside.

I see the woman blush and widely smile as she passes by. I put on my hood and gloves, lower my head, and follow the girl.

She doesn't seem to notice. We walk to her house. When she opens her door, I walk closely behind her. When she wants to shut the door, I quickly put my foot at the doorframe.

The girl doesn't seem to notice. I shut the door behind me. As she takes off her shoes, I take out a piece of wire.

When she's finished, she spins around and faces me. She freezes.

"W-who are you?" she asks me. Her voice shakes. "Get out!"

I shake my head. "I'm sorry. You did something bad. I will be the one punishing you."

She turns around and goes for a run, but I grab her hair and hold the wire around her neck at both ends. She falls onto her knees as she grips the wire. She coughs and coughs as she tries to gasp for air.

I place my foot on her shoulder blades and push her down. The wire cuts her skin.

She stops moving, and the choking stops. Her arms fall next to her body. I let go of the wire. The woman's body drops to the floor. I throw the wire onto her shoes before leaving the house.

I open the door and leave as if nothing has happened. Murder doesn't affect me that much anymore.

I hum as I walk toward Jackson's house.

CHAPTER 9

As I walk toward Jackson's house, I think about the things I've done. I've been following him almost every day. I know his weekly routine and a way to get into his backyard.

What I'm doing is wrong. I shouldn't be doing this. But somehow, I can't stop.

I sigh and shrug as I wave the thoughts away.

When I arrive at Jackson's place, I stop at the door. I look around first and check if anyone's watching me. No one is, so I enter.

"Hey, guys!" I say when I see them on the couch.

Jasmine waves at me. "Hello, Johny boy!"

Jackson waves too, and Alexander just cocks his head with a greeting smile.

I take off my jacket and hang it. I walk to the kitchen and fill a glass with water. "What did I miss?" I ask.

"Peter called for you," Alexander tells me. "He sounded worried."

I turn around to face them. "What?"

I look at my jacket and rush over to it. Digging through my pockets, I look for my phone. When I find it, I quickly unlock it. I have four missed calls and ten unread messages.

I click on a voicemail.

"Hey, John. It's me, Peter. Can you call me back when you get this?" the voicemail says.

I dial his number and call him. He picks up after the first ring. "John?" he answers.

"Peter! Hey! Is everything alright?" I reply.

"What did you do today?" he asks.

I make up a lie as quickly as possible. "I skipped getting coffee and walked in the park. Why?"

Okay, it isn't that good, but it is believable.

"Another murder has happened," Peter tells me. "Marcus called me. The neighbors of the victim called for suspicious actions."

I fall quiet. I look at my friends. They're all watching me. "What's going on?" Jasmine asks me.

"Another murder has happened," I reply.

"Hey, John?" Peter says on the phone. "Everything is alright, okay? You don't have to worry about it."

I shake my head even though he can't see me. "No, this is bad. Do you think it is the man who has killed that other guy?"

Peter falls quiet. I think he's thinking. "Yes, I think it is."

He coughs. I forgot that he's sick.

"Are you alright?" I ask. "Maybe you should leave this to Marcus and the others until you feel better."

Peter coughs another time before answering. "I'm alright, John. No need to worry."

I sigh. "Peter-"

"It's okay. Don't worry, I'll be resting too," Peter reassures me.

I keep quiet for a moment. I hear Peter sigh after two minutes. "John?" he softly asks. "You still there?"

I keep quiet and finally hang up. I put the phone back in my jacket and sit down next to Jackson. They all look at me expectantly.

"There was another murder. Peter will be working further on the case," I tell them.

"You sounded worried," Jackson says. "Is everything alright?"

I shrug. "I'm worried about Peter. He's sick."

Jasmine hugs my arm. "He must be a good friend. You wouldn't be this worried if he wasn't."

I smile. "Peter was there for me. He cares just like you guys. He let me stay at his place even though we only met a few hours ago."

I lower my head. "And I'm in love with him..."

Jasmine leans her head on my shoulder. "John and Peter..." Jasmine starts singing. Alexander and Jackson join the singing. "Sitting in a tree! K.I.S.S.I.N.G!"

I blush and cover my face in embarrassment. "Oh, shut it, guys!"

We laugh it off. Jackson pats my shoulder. "Man, congratulations! You found a lover."

I nod. "The problem is, I don't know how to say it."

Alexander clears his throat and tries to mimic me. "Oh, Peter! You're the love of my life! Please, be my boyfriend!"

We all laugh again. "I swear, you guys will be the death of me!" I laugh.

There are multiple hard knocks on the door. It doesn't stop. Jackson stands up. "Yeah, yeah! I'm coming!"

He walks toward the door, and I throw the keys at him, which he catches perfectly.

He faces the door and opens it.

"Where's he?" I recognize the voice. Peter.

"Uh, he's inside," Jackson answers. He steps aside and lets Peter in. I stand up and walk toward Peter.

"What are you doing here?" I ask.

Peter ignores my question, grabs my shoulders, and pins me against the wall. My heart skips a beat. "P-Peter?"

He points his finger at me. "You don't do that!"

There's anger in his voice. But I sense another tone, concern. "You don't hang up after a silence! You don't don't DON'T!"

With the last word, he bangs his hand against the wall next to my head. My breathing gets faster, and so does my heartbeat.

Peter sighs and steps back. He calms down after a few breaths. "You good?"

I blink multiple times in confusion. I clear my throat and nod.

Peter crosses his arms and nods once. "Sorry about that," he apologizes. "I got mad for a moment."

"I figured that," I reply.

I lean my head against the wall and sink onto the floor.

"You sure you're alright?" Peter asks as he crouches before me.

I nod again. "Yeah, I'm fine."

Lowering my gaze, I bite my lip. "Hey, Peter? Can I ask you something?"

I look up at Peter. He smiles. "Of course, go on."

I look over his shoulder. Jasmine and Alexander hold up their thumbs and mouth: "You can do this!"

I take a deep breath and look straight at Peter. "Peter, do you like..." I can't say it. Peter cocks his head to the left with a sweet smile. "D-do you like...uh...like m-" I just can't say it. "Do you like milk?"

That's... That's it. Someone kill me.

Peter chuckles slightly. "Was that so hard to ask?"

I drown in my shame. Why the fuck did I just ask that?

"I-I just felt awkward asking!" I answer.

Peter smiles widely and messes up my hair as if I was a little boy. "You're adorable. And yes, I like milk. I do prefer chocolate milk."

I smile and lean into his touch. He seems surprised but doesn't mind it. He smiles sweetly at me. "Are you tired again? You shouldn't have skipped coffee just for me."

I shake my head. "Nah, I just like being touched by you."

Peter chuckles. "You're adorable," he says. "Were you-" He holds up his finger and lifts his elbow to his nose. Peter sneezes after a few seconds. He clears his throat. "Woah, a very unexpected sneeze," He says with a soft chuckle. "Sorry about that!"

"That was cute," I suddenly say. I cover my mouth with my hands. "I should not have said that. Uh, you were going to ask something!"

Peter laughs. "You are so bloody adorable! Also, were going to ask something else?"

I blush slightly. My hands luckily cover up my cheeks. I shake my head and reply: "No, nothing."

He shrugs and stands up. "Alright," he says. He holds out his hand. "Need help?"

I smile and take his hand. Peter pulls me off the ground as if I weigh nothing. He's so strong and handsome. Oh, fuck. Why do I keep thinking that? I shake the thoughts off me and look at Peter.

His phone rings. "Oh, one moment," he says as he holds it up. I nod in response. He picks up the call and walks to the kitchen. "With Peter Quintin."

Jackson, Jasmine, and Alexander gather around me.

"Dude, "Do you like milk?" seriously?" Jackson asks me while whispering.

I shrug. "Don't blame me for being embarrassed by expressing my feelings!" I whisper back.

"Couldn't say anything else?" Alexander asks me. "That was damn awkward!"

I feel my face turning red in shame. "Don't remind me of it."

"Chill, guys! It was adorable. At least we know how far John can get," Jasmine defends me.

"Thank you, Jasmine!" I reply.

"I'm sorry, do you mean 'How deep he can fall'?" Jackson teases me.

I sigh. "Okay, guys, this isn't helping at all."

"John!" Peter calls me from the kitchen. He presses his phone against his shoulder. "Marcus wants to talk to you."

I nod and walk over to him. He passes me the phone, and I take it. "Hello?" I answer.

"Hey, John. How are you doing?" Marcus asks me.

"I'm alright," I reply. "I'm a bit worried, though."

Marcus stays quiet. "Worried? About you? Your friends?"

"I'm worried about both. I don't want anything to happen to the people I love," I reply. "If anything happens to them, and it's because that guy wanted me, I would never forgive myself."

There's another silence. Marcus talks again. "If he wanted you? What do you mean by that?"

I keep quiet for a moment. "Is this a questioning over the phone?"

"Yes, it is," Marcus replies. "Do you have a problem with it?"

I swallow. Peter is watching me. He is a cop. I try acting a bit stressed and afraid. "Marcus, how smart do you think the murderer is? W-will he track this phone? Will he find us? Find me? Will he come to kill us next?"

"Woah! Calm down, John. Everything is alright. Take deep breaths," Marcus tells me. "Could you give the phone back to Peter, please?"

I nod and hold out the phone to Peter. He nods once and takes it while looking concerned at me. I slide my hand over my face and let it rest over my mouth in frustration. Peter answers the phone.

I lean against the counter and take deep breaths as I try to calm down. I try to ignore Peter. I take another deep breath and let my shoulders drop.

Peter looks at me and smiles. "Are you okay?" he mouths me.

I smile back and nod. I nod at the phone.

"Are you sure?" Peter mouths me. I nod in response.

"Hey, Marcus. John can talk again," Peter tells Marcus. "Yes, he's fine... No need to worry... Okay, I'll give him the phone."

He holds out the phone to me with a smile. I take it and smile back.

"Hey, it's me again," I say.

"Hey, John. How are you feeling? Calmed down yet?" Marcus asks me.

I nod even though I know he can't see me. "Yeah, I'm fine." I scratch my neck and lower my head. "About earlier..."

"No need to worry, John. I sense that you still feel endangered," Marcus tells me. "Could you tell me how you feel on the streets?"

I hesitate to answer. I look at Peter. He still watches me with full attention.

"I...I don't think I trust people with that information," I finally answer.

Marcus keeps quiet for a moment. I start to question why he does it. "It's okay if you don't want to tell me. It was just a question," Marcus reassures me. "But do know that we're the police. You can trust us with that sort of information."

I sigh and finally answer his question. "I feel watched. When I was at the park, I felt like someone was watching me," I lie. "Every morning, whenever I leave the café, I feel like someone's watching. I'm afraid that someone might attack me one day."

I swallow hard and sigh. "I just don't know what to do... I'm afraid that someone will kill me. That I will be the next victim..."

I turn around and bend over the counter and act frustrated. I rub my eyes and sigh again.

Someone wraps his arms around my chest. I straighten my back slightly and look at my shoulder. Peter places his head on it. "It looked like you needed a hug."

My heartbeat quickens. I smile at Peter. Peter gets closer to the phone and says: "Marcus, let him relax for a moment. He's a bit frustrated. More than a bit."

I chuckle slightly. "Not that frustrated," I say.

"Psh, have you heard how many times you've heavily sighed today? And it's morning!" Peter replies.

I groan in disbelief. "I don't believe you!"

I hear Marcus laugh on the phone. "You two are hilarious. I can see why you two love each other!"

Peter and I fall silent. We both look at each other. I feel my cheeks flush a little. I can't help but see Peter's cheeks turn slightly red too.

"S-sir, John and I are just friends," Peter says.

Marcus falls silent but clears his throat after a few seconds. "Sorry, my bad."

I don't know if I'm imagining it, but I think I feel Peter's arms slightly tighten around my chest.

"Marcus? Could we possibly do the questioning another time?" I ask. "I don't think right now is a good time."

There's this awkward silence again. "I understand," Marcus breaks the silence. "We can do this later. Peter gave me the address where you're staying. I can come by later."

I nod. "Alright. See you later then," I reply.

"See you later. And Peter, how about you stay there? I will come by in a few minutes. It won't be too long," Marcus says. "As long as you don't mind, John."

Peter and I look at each other. We both look at my friends at the same time and then back at each other again.

"I don't mind it," I reply. "What do you think, Peter?"

A smile tugs at the corner of his lips. "Sure, I'll stay. What could go wrong?"

Somehow, I feel relieved he said yes.

"Alright. We'll see each other soon," Marcus says and ends the call.

I close the phone and place it on the counter. Peter doesn't reach out for it yet. Instead, he shuts his eyes as he leans into my neck. I smile and run a hand through his soft hair.

I don't ever want this to end.

I want to kiss him so badly. I want to push him into this counter and kiss him. I want him to throw his arms around my neck and kiss me.

Someone clears his throat, reminding us that we're not alone. Peter clears his throat and lets go of me. I straighten my back and nod awkwardly. We both look at my friends.

"You two should start dating," Alexander says.

My jaw drops to the floor. No, to the other side of the globe.

I can't believe he said that. I awkwardly clear my throat. "W-we're just friends!" I say. "Just friends."

Peter pats my shoulder. With his lips pressed together, he nods once. "Let's just ignore what just happened and wait for Marcus."

"Good idea," I agree. I nod at Peter. "Thee?"

"Yes, please. Thank you," Peter replies.

CHAPTER 10

I go to the cabinet and take a mug. I look at the other cabinet. The's a Post-it with 'John's tea cabinet' written on it. I point at it and look at Jackson. "Jackie, did you do this?" I ask.

He nods and smiles. "Yes, I indeed did, John."

I shake my head while a smile tugs at the corner of my lips. I open the cabinet and get out a pot of dried elderberry flowers. When I get the jar, I get out a small tea contraption. When I have everything, I shut the cabinet and place everything on the counter behind me.

I see Peter watching me with full attention. I smile at him. "What do you think?" I ask him.

He looks at me with a smile and leans against the counter. "Impressive, very impressive. You're a tea expert," he replies.

I shrug as I chuckle. "You have seen me drink coffee multiple times. I do like a cup of tea from time to time."

Someone clears their throat. Peter and I look at my friends.

"Every," Jasmine says.

"Single," Alexander continues.

"Day!" Jackson finishes.

I feel my cheeks flush again. "Oh, please, I don't do this every day."

Peter pats my shoulder. "Says the man with a whole collection of tea in the cabinet."

All of us laugh a bit.

I look at Peter. "Would you like to assist me?" I ask. "You don't have to."

Peter smiles and nods. "What would you like me to do?"

I gesture to the stove. "Do you mind boiling the water?"

"It doesn't sound like a hard task," Peter says.

With an evil grin, I turn around to the drawers. "Wait until you see, my dear friend."

"Uh-oh!" I hear Jackson shout. "Tea expert in action!"

I open the drawer and take out a thermometer. With a smile, I turn around and hold it up.

Everyone gathers around the counter. Peter's facial expression has changed. He looks confused with a hint of expectation. The other looked at me with pure confusion. I can't help but chuckle at their reaction.

"Peter, I want you to boil the water and keep it between 170 and 190 degrees Fahrenheit," I tell Peter. "Not higher, not lower, please."

I see Peter's eyes widen as he presses his lips together. He takes the thermometer and takes a good look at it. "Okay, in a moment," he says after a few seconds.

There's knocking on the door. I take my eyes off the jar of dried flowers.

"I'll get it!" Jasmine says with a smile. She turns around and hops toward the door.

I turn around to see what Peter is doing. Peter has already put the water on the stove. I watch the water and the fire underneath.

I reach out to one of the buttons. Peter does the same. Our hands touch. For a moment, we looked at each other. I pull my hand back and smile a bit shyly. I lower my gaze and awkwardly scratch my neck. "Sorry," I say. "I thought it would be better to turn it on a bit higher."

"I had the same thought," Peter replies.

"Peter! John!" Jasmine shouts at us. "There's a man at the door. Marcus Anderson is his name."

Peter and I turn around. Marcus steps inside and waves as he says: "Hello, John. Hello, Peter."

"Good morning, Marcus," Peter and I say together.

I clear my throat awkwardly and turn back to the boiling water. I hear Peter chuckle. "Well, someone's a bit shy," Peter says.

I bump into his elbow and reply: "Oh, shut up. It's not my fault this is awkward."

I turn on the stove a bit more and let the water cook. "Marcus, would you like some tea?" I ask Marcus without looking back.

I hear him take off his jacket. "That would be nice, thank you."

With a smile, I put the thermometer into the water and see how hot it is. "Perfect," I say under my breath.

Peter chuckles as he watches me work over my shoulder. I hear Marcus come closer too.

I get the pot off the stove and turn it off. "Be careful! Hot pot!" I shout as I turn to the counter. "Peter, could you get more mugs from the cabinet?"

"Yes, no problem," he says as he turns to the cabinet. "Who wants tea?"

"You, Marcus," I look at my friends. "Anyone?"

They all nod their head. "Let's see how good your tea is!" Jackson says.

"Alright. Jackson, Jasmine, Alexander, Marcus, you, and me," I tell Peter. "Meaning four more mugs."

"Alrighty! Four more mugs for the guys!" Peter says as he takes out the mugs.

"And woman!" Jasmine shouts.

"And woman!" Peter repeats as he places them on the counter.

I chuckle and pour the boiling water into the mugs. I turn around and place the pot back on the stove. "So, Marcus. What are the questions you've got?" I ask as I turn back to my tea cabinet.

"Are you sure you want to answer them now?" Marcus asks me.

"Yes, I'm sure. I relax when I'm busy with tea. The smell and work are calming," I reply. "This is a good moment for the questioning."

I take out a couple more tea contraptions. I turn back to the tea. "Please, go ahead and ask us the questions.'

I see Marcus nod and take out a small notebook. "As you wish. Since when did all this start?"

"This all started the day my girlfriend broke up with me," I answer as I open the jar of dried elderberry flowers. "That was the day I met Peter."

I hold it under my nose and smell the aroma. I hold it out to Peter. He looks a bit confused. I chuckle as he takes the jar. "Smell it," I instruct him.

Peter chuckles slightly before smelling it. I see his eyes widen very slightly. "Woah, it smells amazing."

I smile, satisfied by his reaction. I nod at Marcus. He shrugs and takes the jar. He also takes a sniff. "Oh, yeah, that's good."

I laugh slightly and look at my friends. They shake their heads. I shrug and take the jar back. "Go on," I tell Marcus as I put the dried flowers in the tea contraptions.

"Alright. Could you tell me everything you remember from your attack?" Marcus asks me.

I nod and put the tea contraptions into the water. "It is a male. I wasn't able to see his face. I don't remember the voice either," I answer his question. I give everyone their mugs. "Wait a bit before you drink."

They thank me and take the mugs closer. Marcus writes things down in his notebook. "Can you tell me what happened?"

"I remember hearing crying in an alley. Walking toward the noise, it suddenly stopped," I say. "I remember that I got hit in the back of the head. Then I woke up tied to a chair with tape over my mouth. I already told the rest."

I take out teaspoons and give everyone one. I take one for myself and stir the tea slowly. I smile as the heat hits my face. The scent of the tea slowly fills the room.

Peter gently bumps my arm. I look at him. "I guess I'm not the only one who often gets lost in their thoughts," he says with a wide smile.

I blush slightly from embarrassment. "I-I'm sorry! Did someone say something?"

Everyone laughs slightly. I feel like sinking into the ground and never coming back to breathe.

"I guess your head is in the clouds," Marcus tells me.

I chuckle awkwardly. "My head's on my shoulders. I was thinking about the tea."

"You're right," Marcus replies. "Tea really relaxes you."

I smile at the mug. "Yes, it does. Anyways, what did you say?"

"Do you know any other information?" Marcus asks.

I squint my eyes and think for a moment. What can I add?

"The clothes he wore were black. The clothes were a black hood, pants, and a mask," I say. "The room was dark with only one light focused on the first victim."

Marcus writes everything down. A couple of minutes have passed now. I take out the tea contraptions from the mugs and place them on some paper tissues.

Marcus clicks with his pen. The sound fades away as I get lost in my thoughts. I shut my eyes, hold the mug close to my nose, and smell the goods.

I shouldn't have murdered those people. But somehow, it felt good. They all wanted to take Peter away from me.

Sometimes I wonder what his body looks like. I've seen his chest but never down there.

I blow slightly before taking a sip of the tea. The sweet liquid meets my tongue. I smile.

I look up from my mug. Everyone stares at me. I almost spit out the tea. Coughing, I place the cup back on the counter and cover my mouth.

"Why does this always happen to me?" I ask, half coughing.

They start laughing at me. I cover my flushed face with my hands.

Why am I always the victim of humiliation?

I clear my throat. "Okay, Okay. I know what it looks like, but I am not high!"

Jackson crouches as he laughs. Jasmine holds onto Alexander for dear life. Marcus and Peter laugh together.

"Okay! My embarrassment isn't that funny!" I shout. "What about Jackosn who...Uh... Or Jasmine who- Alexander who... Okay, I give up!"

They all continue to laugh. I take a deep breath and quietly die from embarrassment. I look at Peter for a moment.

Peter cocks his head up and smiles. "Alright, I will end your suffering," he says. "Tea is good for certain things, right? What's this tea good for?"

Everyone goes quiet and looks at Peter and then at me. I smile and take the jar of dried flowers. "In this jar, there are dried elderberry flowers. You can also use fresh ones," I start. "Elderberry tea," I continue while looking at Peter. "Is good for colds which you have."

Peter chuckles slightly and scratches the back of his neck. "Oh, John. You're too kind!"

I smile and gesture to their mugs. "Go on. You haven't drunk it yet."

Everyone takes their mugs and takes a sip of their tea. I do the same. I watch them expectantly.

Peter lowers his mug and licks his lips. "Woah! That's what I call a good drink."

"I agree with Peter. The tea tastes amazing," Marcus says.

I smile, satisfied. I look at my friends for their reaction. The nod, agreeing. "Alright, now I know why you're obsessed with tea," Alexander says.

I chuckle slightly. "I'm glad you all like the tea," I say.

Marcus places the mug down. He clears his throat. Everyone turns to him. "I want to ask a question to you all. You have to be sure before answering."

"Sure, ask away," Jackson replies.

"Would you guys be willing to help with the case?" Marcus asks us. His tone is serious.

Peter places his mug down on the counter. He looks sternly at Marcus. "Marcus! Are you seriously asking them to help us with a murder case?" he asks.

Marcus looks back at Peter. "Yes, I just did," Marcus replies. "They could help us."

"No! Have you seen how John reacted to the first murder? He's a victim!" Peter shouts. "Who knows what will happen next?"

"That's why I added to be sure about it!" Marcus replies.

"You can't-"

"I'm in!" I shout.

Before Peter could finish, I said it. Peter looks at me. His facial expression changed into a more concerning expression. "John? Are you serious?" he asks me.

I nod at him with a confident smile. "Yes, I'm sure," I reply.

Jackson raises his hand. "I'm in too!"

The rest raise their hands too. "We're in too!"

Peter looks at all of us and rests his gaze on me. He sighs before saying: "Fine. Remember, this is your choice. Step out anytime you want."

I smile and him and nod. "Drink your tea. If you cough, I will make more and force you to drink it."

Peter laughs slightly. "Funny."

He takes his mug and finishes his tea. We all do the same.

It's nighttime. The boys and Jasmine already went to bed. Marcus, Peter, and I are sitting around the dinner table. Marcus has his files with him.

"So, you guys are going to be working with us," Marcus begins. "Peter will be looking out for you with another agent. The other agent's name is Hugo Danvers."

Peter groans slightly. "Danvers? Really? You know I dislike him!"

"And that's exactly why I want him with you," Marcus says.

"Why?" I ask.

"Why do I hate him, or why did Marcus put him with us?" Peter asks me.

"Both," I reply.

"I put Officer Danvers with you because Peter needs to learn to work with the people he dislikes," Marcus answers.

Peter sighs. "And I hate him because he's mean."

Marcus scoffs. "He's not mean!"

"Yes, he is!" Peter replies. "He threw a glass at my head once!"

"He what?" I ask, surprised.

They both fall silent. Marcus breaks the silence by saying: "He was in a bad mood that day."

Peter laughs sarcastically. "In a bad mood?" he asks. "So the times he threw coffee on my shirt and tripped me, was him being in a bad mood?"

Marcus sighs. "Let's just shut up about it. You're going to work with him whether you like it or not."

Peter groans once again. "This sucks," he mouths to me.

It makes me laugh. Marcus clears his throat. "Alright, back to business. You'll be meeting him tomorrow morning in the café."

"What?" Peter asks with a hint of anger. "So he'll be ruining our coffee time?"

I sigh and shake my head with a small smile. "Peter," I say, gently kicking his leg under the table. "We'll have plenty of time alone."

Peter looks at me and down at our legs. I feel my cheeks flush and look away.

"It's just... Our coffee moment is our moment," Peter says. "It's not the coffee that gets me going in the morning. It's you."

I look at him again. "And you said I was adorable."

Peter chuckles. We both look each other right in the eyes. "That's because you're a clumsy puppy," he says.

Marcus clears his throat, reminding us that he's there too. We both look at him. "You sure you two aren't dating?" he asks with a mischievous smile.

I cross my arms on the table, place my head in them, and die of embarrassment.

Marcus laughs.

"Marcus! We're just friends!" Peter shouts in defense.

"Peter, John, just kiss already!" Marcus teases us.

Marcus seems to be the only one who's able to laugh. Peter and I are just dying of embarrassment.

Peter puts his hands up. "Alright! I'm going to use the restroom!" he says as he gets up. He looks at me, and I point at the door across Jackson's bedroom.

As Peter leaves, Marcus's attention is on me. When we hear the bathroom door shut, he asks: "You're in love with him, aren't you?"

I feel like sinking into my chair. "Y-yes," I stutter, embarrassed.

Marcus chuckles slightly.

"H-how did you know?" I ask him.

"Well, I'm a detective," Marcus answers. "And it's obvious. But about Peter, he doesn't know whether someone like likes him or not."

I nod. "Yeah, I've noticed it too."

Marcus nods and turns serious. He gestures to the files. "The two murders that have happened seemed to be people who love Peter," he says. "I'm kind of worried about you."

I take a deep breath and bite my lip. My hands are fidgeting under the table as I look at the files.

Marcus seems to notice. "You're afraid that something might happen, aren't you?"

I nod in response, keeping my lips pressed together.

The door opens. "I heard you were talking shit about me!" Peter shouts as he comes hopping to the table.

My heart skips a beat. Oh, shit.

He laughs slightly. "Sorry, I've always wanted to do that!"

I exhale in relief. "Haha, very funny!" I say as calmly as possible.

Peter sits back down at the table and points at the files. "So, about tomorrow morning..."

"No, you're going to stick with him whether you like it or not!" Marcus interrupts him.

Peter groans, and I chuckle slightly.

"Alright, tomorrow morning. I'll be waiting in front of the café as always," I say.

CHaPTer 11

The following morning arrives. I get up and put on my clothes. I walk toward Jackson's room and quietly look inside. They're still asleep. I smile as I close the door.

I walk to the front door, put on my shoes, and go outside. The clouds are grey. I have the feeling it will rain soon.

On my way to the café, there's a comforting breeze following. Birds chirp beautifully in the morning. People are opening their shops. We greet each other.

I arrive at the café. I don't see Peter or any officer-looking person. I shrug and wait for them at the entrance.

Ten minutes pass by. Peter's never late. Maybe they got into a fight on the way. I quietly hum as I continue to wait for them.

Suddenly, I hear two males shouting at each other. I look in their direction. It's Peter with a man. It's a man who's slightly taller than Peter and has short blonde hair. Peter wears a jacket and keeps his hands in his pockets.

I wave a bit at them. Peter waves back at me.

"Hey!" I shout as they come closer.

"Hi!" Peter shouts back.

We stand awkwardly at the entrance. I clear my throat and gesture at the man next to him. "So, are you Hugo Danvers?" I ask the man.

The man smiles and me and holds out his hand. "Indeed I am. Pleasure meeting you. You must be John Welling."

I shake his hand. "Please, the pleasure is mine."

Peter clears his throat. We both look at him. "Coffee?" he asks.

I smile and nod in response. The three of us enter the café.

"I'll go get our coffee," Peter tells us. He nods at Hugo and looks back at me. "Go get to know his ass a bit better."

I chuckle softly. I look at Hugo and down at my feet. "Sorry, I found it funny..." I apologize softly.

Someone places a hand on my shoulder. It startles me. Someone laughs. "You're adorable," Hugo says.

Peter gently bumps my elbow. "Latte?" he asks me. I nod.

Hugo clears his throat, probably wanting me to say something.

I look at him, turn, and walk to a seat in silence. I hear Peter and Hugo talk before Hugo comes to sit next to me.

I look at my hands under the table in silence. I can feel Hugo's gaze upon me. He sighs and breaks the silence. "Sorry if I was rude when I called you adorable," he says.

I shrug and reply: "It's alright."

There's another awkward silence.

"You're not much of a talker, are you?" Hugo asks me.

I shrug again. "I'm clumsy, and caring, I get nervous quickly, and I'm weird. Perhaps other things, but I don't know."

I see him press his lips together. We stay quiet again.

"Why does he hate you?" I finally ask him when I have the courage. I look at him.

He shrugs. "I guess it's because we started on the wrong foot."

Peter comes and sits next to us. He gives me my latte and smiles. Peter passes Hugo his coffee without a word. I hold my cup under the table and look at it.

"So, what did you two talk about?" Peter asks us. He places his hand on top of my cup to get my attention. I look at him. He whispers: "Don't crush your cup this time."

I nod with a smile. I place the cup on the table and keep my hands under the table again.

"So, he's quiet," Hugo says. He crosses his arms on the table. "That's cute."

"Please, don't call me cute," I tell him quickly. I start playing with my band-aids under the table.

"Danvers, do me a favor and shut that big ass hole of yours," Peter says, his tone aggressive.

I see Hugo roll his eyes as he groans.

I want to grab my cup but stop and slam my hand on the table. I just pulled off a Band-Aid. I press my lips together as it starts to burn.

Peter pats my back. "That must've hurt..."

I groan and sink into my chair. I grab my coffee and take a sip.

"Wait!" Peter shouts. He was too late. I place my cup back on the table and bite my lip. I forgot to blow again.

"Okay, John. Quick question, are you nervous?" Peter asks me.

I clear my throat and nod my head. I take a deep breath. I see Peter glare at Hugo.

Hugo looks at me. "Uhm...John? Are you alright?"

Peter clears his throat. "Oh, I'm sorry, I don't think I was clear enough. Shut. The. Fuck. Up."

Hugo slams his hand on the table. "You don't get to shut me up, dick-head!

Peter laughs sarcastically. "Oh, wow! I'm so sorry! Are you going to throw things at my head again? Perhaps your last remaining brain cell?"

"Hey!" Danger gets up and hits Peter on the head. Peter stands up and starts shouting at him.

I can only watch them. My body doesn't want to respond.

As they argue, they push each other. Hugo grabs his cup and tries to throw the coffee on Peter. Peter holds Hugo's arm back to prevent it from happening. Danvers drops the cup. It hits the table. The hot liquid splatters onto my wound.

I stand up quickly, causing the chair to fall back. The two go quiet.

"Oh, geez... John, are you alright?" Peter asks. He steps closer to help, but I stop him.

"P-Peter, stay back, please. I-I will be taking my leave. Sorry," I say. I turn round and run outside. I hear the two call out my name.

I'm lucky I'm a fast runner. I rush to the police station.

The coffee on my wound starts to burn. When I'm at the police station, I rush inside and go to the counter. "Marcus Anderson! I'm looking for Detective Marcus Anderson!" I shout. I'm out of breath. My throat has gotten dry.

"Sir, what happened? What happened to your arm?" the officer from behind the counter asks me. She wants to have a closer look at my wound, but I pull my arm away.

"Please, I'm just looking for Detective Marcus Anderson," I say. With my trembling hands, I take out a tissue and grab a pen from the officer. I wrote down Marcus's phone number.

The officer takes it and dials the number on the phone on the corner of the counter. The phone rings three times before he picks up.

"With Marcus Anderson," Marcus says.

"Yes, Mr. Anderson. There's a man here who wants to see you," the officer says. "I'll ask him."

The officer looks at me. "Could you tell me your name, please?"

I nod. "I'm John. John Welling," I reply.

The officer smiles at me before talking back to the phone. "He says his name is John Welling."

She nods. "Alright... We're in the lobby of the police station."

I turn around and look at the entrance doors. I hear the officer hang up, so I turn back to her.

"Mr. Anderson will be here in a few minutes," she says. "Do you mind telling me what happened?"

I nod in response. "I'm working on a case with multiple police officers. I just met one in the café with someone I already knew. I got nervous and got hot coffee on my wound. I couldn't take it anymore, so I ran."

The officer gives me a sympathetic smile. She holds out her hand. "Do you mind it if I see your wound?" she asks softly.

I nod a bit hesitantly. I hold out my arm.

She takes a good look at it. "Hmm... Do you know Peter Quintin?"

She looks up at me. I look away.

"No worries. I'm just asking because we're working on a case," she says. She nods once at my wound. "That looks exactly like the wound one of the victims has."

"O-oh..." I softly say. I feel a bit embarrassed. "I'm a victim, and I know Peter. Do you work with Hugo Danvers too?"

She nods with a smile. "Indeed I do. I do dislike the idea of Peter and Hugo working together. They're rivals."

I chuckle quietly. "Yeah, I've noticed..."

"Oh, you poor soul. Is this because of them arguing?" she asks.

I nod in response. "Y-yeah... I'm not used to Peter shouting. It was a huge surprise too."

I force a smile and look down at my hands. The officer places a hand on mine. I look at her. She smiles. "I'm Anastasia Higgs. Since we'll be working together, I can help you get through this. Everything will be okay."

Her gaze goes over my shoulder. I look behind me. Marcus walks toward us, his coat soaking wet. I knew it was raining. He takes it off and asks: "What happened? Were they being mean? Are you alright?"

I nod and pull my arm back. Anastasia smiles at me.

"Well...yeah. Hugo and Peter started arguing in the café," I begin. "Hugo called me cute and made me feel nervous. When Peter tried to comfort me, Hugo talked and made Peter mad by doing so."

Marcus sighs and nods. He looks at my arm. "You're scratching aga-" His eyes widen slightly. "Did you burn yourself?"

I look down at my arms. I let my sleeve cover my forearm and put my hands in my pockets. "It's nothing to worry about!"

Marcus reaches out to my hand. "May I have a look?"

I hesitate slightly. Marcus quietly says: "I won't force you to do anything. You can say no."

I shake my head and keep my arm close to my body.

The door flies open. We all turn to it. Peter starts choking the fuck out of Hugo on the floor.

Hugo grasps Peter's hands, trying to break free while trying to get every bit of air possible.

Marcus runs over to them and pulls Peter away. Peter starts fighting back, his teeth gritting as he does.

"You don't fucking dare to touch him!" Peter starts shouting. "Touch him, and I'll kill you! I'll skin you, tear you apart, anything!"

Hugo gasps for air and crawls away from Peter. Anastasia helps Hugo by pulling him to the counter. Multiple officers help Marcus to calm Peter down. I, on the other hand, am nailed to the ground.

My breathing quickens, and so does my heartbeat. I try to get my mind straight, but there are too many things happening.

My head starts to feel light-headed as I try to catch my breath. I've never seen Peter this angry.

Peter glances over at me. His eyes filled with anger. His hands form clenching fists. I see the nail marks on the palms of his hands. His face slightly softens as he senses something going on.

He tries breaking free again, his gaze on me. My knees buckle, and I fall onto the floor. Every noise fades away, I see Anastasia crawling toward me, and then everything goes black.

Slowly, I open my eyes. I'm lying on the floor. A voice becomes clear as seconds pass by. It's Peter's voice. He's kneeling beside me.

"John? Can you hear me? Can you hear me, John?" he asks continuously. There's a hint of concern in his tone.

I feel like closing my eyes again. I feel nauseous and dizzy. What just happened?

I swallow before asking: "What just happened to me?"

Peter sighs in relief. He helps me sit up with my back against the counter. Marcus and Anastasia are on the other side next to me. Hugo is standing from a small distance. He still looks worried, though.

"I'm so sorry," Peter apologizes. "I didn't realize what this was doing to you. What I was doing to you."

I smile at him. "Don't worry, Peter. I'm alright, just a bit light-headed."

I look to my right. Anastasia smiles at me. Her dark green eyes look into my eyes. Her wavy ginger hair falls down her shoulders as she holds out my hand to Marcus.

Peter follows my gaze and looks at my bruised skin. "Oh, God... I'm so sorry! We- I-" He falls quiet. I see his eyes water.

I gently pull my hand away. I throw my arms around Peter and hold him tightly against me. He hugs me tightly.

We stay quiet as we hug, and so does the rest.

I quietly take a good sniff of Peter's scent. He still smells magnificent. I run a hand through his wet fluffy hair. His forehead feels slightly warm due to his fever.

Peter pulls back and wipes away a tear. "Sorry," he says.

I chuckle slightly. "And you called me cute."

He scoffs. "Very funny, Cheesecake!"

I laugh. "Cheesecake? Why?"

"Well, you're soft, sweet, and adorable!"

"Since when is a cheesecake adorable?"

"Have you ever seen those fluffy small cakes? Some have drawings on them, and they are adorable!"

"You're so weird! I will call you something too! Pudding!"

Peter laughs. "Pudding? Like Harley Quinn calls the Joker? Not bad for a Cheesecake!"

I stick out my tongue and chuckle along.

Someone clears their throat. We all look at Hugo. "I'm sorry for making you feel bad earlier, John," he apologizes.

I smile and nod. "It's alright," I say. "You are forgiven. But please, don't call me adorable or any other things."

He smiles and nods as he agrees.

I look back at Peter. "Help me up, will you?"

He chuckles and stands up, offering a hand to me. I take his hand, and he helps me up. I need some time before being able to stand straight. I'm still a bit dizzy. Peter helps me not fall over.

Marcus and Anastasia stand up too. "John? How do you feel?" Marcus asks me.

"Just a bit light-headed, nothing too bad," I reply. I'm finally able to stand up by myself. "When are we going to talk about the case?"

I look at Marcus. He seems to be a bit unsure. "Are you sure you want to talk about now?" he asks, his tone concerned.

I smile reassuringly at him and nod once.

He nods back at me and gestures to a door. "Then let's go to the office."

CHAPTER 12

We follow Marcus into an office.

There's a whiteboard hanging on one side of the room. There are pictures of the murdered people and places. There are multiple desks in the room. There is a stack of files on one desk.

They let me look around. I walk toward the files. I take a look at them. The first victim's name was George Harold, the bar guy.

He got killed by getting hit by a pipe. There were no fingerprints, no faces, and no witnesses. I turn to the next page. There's a picture of the dead body. I don't know if I should be happy or disgusted.

I shut the file. I open the other.

The second victim's name was Iliana Henry. She got killed by getting choked with a wire. There again were no fingerprints, no faces, and no witnesses. I turn to the next page to see the dead body. Her skin is pale, her eyes looking into the void, and there is a mark of the wire on her neck.

I shut the file and put it on top of George Harold's. I look at another file, the murderer's file. I open it.

There is no name and no picture. His information is unknown. There are the deaths of the people he murdered.

I don't know how I feel about it. The cops have a file of an unknown murderer. Only one person in this room knows the man, me.

I close the file and place it on top of the two others. The last file lies before me. I'm not sure if I want to open it since I already know what's inside.

I take a deep breath and open it anyway. John Welling, alive. It feels weird knowing that they have two files about me. One file is innocent, and the other is as cruel as can be.

I shut the file as I already knew everything. I walk over to the whiteboard. The pictures of the victims are on it.

I turn to the rest. "Is this everything?" I ask them.

"Yes, this is everything. It may not be a lot, but that guy is good," Marcus says. "He knows what to do. He doesn't leave anything behind except the body and the weapon. No fingerprints nor footprints."

I nod. I have no idea if I should take that as a compliment. I look back at the whiteboard. I hear someone step closer. It's Hugo.

"How do you feel about seeing all these dead people?" he asks me curiously.

I shrug in response. "I have no idea. I don't feel disgusted or afraid anymore. I can look at it as if it were in a movie."

I see Hugo nod in the corner of my eye. I look at Peter. He's staring at the files of Iliana Henry. "I used to know her," he says as if he could sense my gaze. He looks at me. "She was a friend of mine."

"I'm sorry," I pity him. I realize that what I do can hurt the person I adore the most. What can I do to cheer him up?

He forces a small smile. "It's alright. It's not your fault."

I shake my head and start acting. "If only I could just remember his face or had stopped him when he let me go. Maybe she would have been alive."

I clench my hands into trembling fists. "Then all of this would have ended quicker! If I wasn't such a weak fool, she would've been alive! Maybe George Harold would've been alive too!"

Peter rushes over to me and pulls me in. "It's not your fault, John!" he shouts. He presses my head into his shoulder.

I force tears to roll down my cheeks. I sob softly. "I'm sorry, I'm sorry, I'm sorry..."

Marcus and Anastasia come closer, but Peter gives them a sign to be quiet. Hugo stays from a distance since he knows that Peter could get angry again.

"John, nothing of this is your fault," Marcus reassures me. "You couldn't do anything."

We all stay quiet as I sob into Peter's shoulder. Peter runs a gentle hand through my hair. He whispers: "Say it until you believe it. Say that it wasn't your fault."

I take a deep breath before continuously saying: "It wasn't my fault."

I calmed down after saying it a few times. I let myself sink into Peter's embrace.

I try to say something funny to show that I feel better. "Now we just have to hope that I don't get sick because of you."

Peter chuckles slightly. I feel his arms slightly tighten around me. "Even after all this, you still know how to smile."

We don't pull away from each other. We hug each other for a while longer.

We can hear Anastasia make an 'Aww' sound. Peter and I pull away quickly and awkwardly nod at each other. The rest starts to laugh.

I feel like sinking into the ground from embarrassment again.

Marcus clears his throat. We all look at him. "How about we work on the case another time? I think we all have other work to do."

Marcus winks at Anastasia. She cocks her head in confusion. She looks at her watch, and her eyes widen. "Oh, fuck! Thank you, Mr. Anderson!" she shouts. She turns around and runs outside.

"Oh, yeah! She has a date!" Peter says. "I totally forgot about that."

Marcus chuckles slightly. "How about you three try to get along with each other?" he suddenly asks. "I'm not saying that you have to, but it would be better."

Peter groans again. I playfully hit his bicep. "And you said that I sigh a lot in the morning!"

Peter gasps dramatically. "Oh! How dare you!"

Peter and I start laughing.

I look at Hugo. "As much as I would like to get to know you, I have things to do."

"And perhaps you should brush your teeth, Danvers," Peter says. "Your breath smells like onions."

Peter scoffs, and we both leave the room. Peter throws his arm around my neck as we walk outside. I feel my cheeks flush.

As we reach the entrance, we stop at the doors. The rain has stopped. Peter and I look each other in the eyes. We smile.

"So, what's that thing you have to do?" he asks me.

I chuckle and shrug his arm off what I actually didn't want to do. "Well, that's a secreto!"

Peter's eyes widen slightly. "Did you just finish your sentence in Spanish?"

"Just so you know, my brother lives in Spain," I reply.

Peter scoffs. "You never told me you had a brother, nor tell me you could speak Spanish fluently!"

I start to laugh, Peter chuckles. "So, what else can you say?"

"No hay nadie como tú (there's no one like you)!" I say.

Peter squints his eyes. "And that means?"

"Figure it out!" I shout. I push him playfully and run outside. I hear Peter burst out in laughter.

He doesn't follow and lets me go.

I've been thinking about what I could do to cheer Peter up after I killed Iliana. I walk past a store. I wonder if Peter likes flowers and chocolate.

I shrug, take my chances, and walk into the flower shop. I put on my gloves. The aroma of flowers fills my nose. The flowers have multiple colors.

Someone walks over to me. It seems to be a worker. "Hello, can I help you with anything, sir?" he asks me, smiling brightly.

I smile back and nod. "I'm just looking around for flowers for my friend."

"Ah, for a friend. Is it a confession, as a secret admirer, or anything else?"

I feel my cheeks flush. "Secret admirer..." I mumble quietly.

The florist chuckles. "That's adorable."

I clear my throat and nod. "Do you happen to have purple Hyacinths?" I ask him.

He nods and gestures to a corner where there are multiple Hyancinths. I take a look at them. I look at the darkest purple they have. "These are perfect," I say. "I'll take these."

The florist nods with a smile. "Good choice. Do you know what they mean?"

I nod and answer: "They present guilt."

The florist nods. "That's correct. How many do you want?"

"Four will do, thank you," I reply.

He nods and takes out four flowers. "Want it in a bouquet?" he asks me.

"Just a ribbon, please," I reply.

He nods and takes out a red ribbon. He ties the flowers together. He passes me the flowers and says: "That would be nine dollars, please."

I nod with a smile and give him the money. I thank him and leave the store with the flowers.

I walk to the other side of the street. There's a candy shop. I enter it.

Children run around the shop. I chuckle as someone bumps into me. "Sorry!" she apologizes with the sweetest voice.

"That's alright, little one!" I reply, petting her head slightly.

Her mother calls: "Rosemary! Be careful!" She looks apologizingly at me. "Sorry about her. She's a wild one."

"It's alright, no problem."

The little girl starts running around again. Her mother sighs and gets after her.

I walk toward the counter where they sell all sorts of chocolates. I take a white box filled with twenty small dark chocolates.

I buy it and go to Peter's house. He's home. I'm wearing my black clothes and have my face covered. I leave the gifts on his doorstep with a note.

Dear, PeterHere are some gifts for you. Since I murdered your friend, I thought this would make it up to you.- your secret admirer

I ring his doorbell and start running as fast as possible. Peter opens the door. He saw me. He shouts out for me. I keep running without looking back.

CHAPTER 13

I ran home. I open the door. Alexander and Jasmine are kissing on the couch.

They stop just like me. We look at each other. I scoff. "About damn time you guys kissed!"

I can hear Jackson burst out in laughter in the kitchen. I see Alexander and Jasmine blush.

"And it's about damn time you and Peter kiss!" Jasmine shouts at me.

I feel my seeks flush as she mentions Peter and I kissing. "S-shut up!" I shout back.

Jackson falls to the ground from laughter. Alexander starts laughing too, and so does Jasmine.

My phone starts ringing. I pick it up. It's Peter.

"Peter?" I ask.

"John! Police station, now!"

Before I can answer, he hangs up.

I sigh and put it in my pockets. "I have to go, sorry."

I reach for the door, but Jackson calls my name. I turn to him. "John! Don't work too hard, alright?"

I smile and nod. "Of course."

I leave the house and go to the police station.

When I arrive at the police station, I head toward the room I went to this morning.

The four were waiting for me. It's like walking into the wrong classroom. All eyes are on me.

"John," Peter says. He walks over to me and grabs me by my shoulders. "Where were you?"

"I was at home," I reply. "Why?"

Marcus throws the flowers on the table. "Guilt," he says. "These flowers present guilt. The murderer wrote a note and called himself a secret admirer."

"Were you followed?" Hugo asks me.

I shake my head. Peter lets go of my shoulders and sighs. "This guy knows where I live."

"Looks like you have a stalker, Peter," Hugo says.

"You call me Mr. Quintin at work, Danvers!" Peter shouts at him. He sounds angry.

"Hey! Keep your fucking voice down!" Hugo hisses back.

Peter steps toward Danvers at a fast pace. He points his finger at him. "Keep your mouth shut, Danvers! You're not the one with a bloody stalker!"

Hugo clenches his hands into fists. "You only want attention because of it!"

"Shut up! Both of you!" Anastasia shouts at them.

They both ignore her and continue to shout at each other. "I bet you did all those murders just to get attention from everyone!" Hugo shouts.

Peter seems to be angrier than ever. It's like something snapped in him. He raises his fist and punches Hugo in the face.

Marcus comes between them. Anastasia pulls Peter away from Hugo, while Marcus does the same with Hugo.

Peter keeps wanting to hurt Hugo. His teeth grit together, and his nails leave marks on his palms as he clenches them into fists.

Anastasia shouts at me for help. I don't move a muscle. Anastasia grabs Peter's head and forces him to look at me. He stays still for a moment.

I can't take it anymore and go for a run. I hear Peter call out my name. I turn around the corner. I run into the restroom. I put on my gloves and turn on the sink.

In the halls, they call out my name. I stay quiet and hidden. I wait for the sink to fill.

Hugo runs into the restroom. "Oh! John! Oh, God. I found you," he says, half panting.

"Yeah, you found me," I mumble, my tone a bit disappointed.

Hugo sighs deeply. "Look, I'm sorry I was so mad earlier."

I scoff. "No, you aren't."

I look at the sink. It's full. "Why do you hate Peter?"

"You already asked that question," Hugo answers.

"Why do you hate Peter?" I repeat.

He sighs. "Alright, what do you want?"

I point at the sink. Confused, Hugo looks at it. He looks back at me and then at my hands. "Why are you wearing gloves?" he asks.

I chuckle slightly. "You were so mean to Peter," I say. "I think you deserve punishment."

Then the realization hit him. I step toward him and crack my knuckles. "Let's get this over with."

I try grabbing him by his collar, but he grabs my wrist and turns me around. I begin to laugh. I look in the mirror. He seems scared. "It looks like I scared a puppy!" I shout.

I turn myself around and kick him in the stomach. He gasps as he grasps the spot where I hit him. "What is wrong with you?" he asks aggressively.

I shrug. "I just love Peter so much that I would kill for him, literally. Now, I can badly injure you, or I could spare you the pain and just kill you."

"You monster!"

He gets ready to throw another punch. I step aside as he throws his body forward. I take his wrist and trip him. I hold his arm back and place my foot there. He groans in pain.

"Shall I break it? Hm... Yes."

I stamp my leg on his forearm with all the strength I have. He cries out as the sound of cracking bones fills the room.

I grab him by his hair and hold him near the water. "Final words?"

"You. Are. A. Monster!" he yells.

"Good choice," I say, pushing his head underwater. Bubbles float to the surface. Hugo struggles and tries to get as much air as possible. For fun, I lift his head. He gasps for air. In the middle of his breath, I plunge him back into the water.

After a few minutes of him struggling, his movements lessen to a stop. I keep his head underwater for a few minutes longer before letting go.

I open the window. I take Hugo's necktie, dip it in a bit of water, and stuff it into my mouth. I hit my head against the wall, causing my nose to bleed. I let myself fall into one of the stalls. I pretend to be panicking and lean against the wall. I start screaming.

After a minute or five, an officer rushes into the room. He looks at Hugo first and then at me. He kneels before me and takes out the necktie.

I tremble and start coughing.

"I need help in the male restroom of hall seven!" the officer speaks into his communication device. He turns back to me and lets me rest against the wall. He gives me a tissue for my bleeding nose. "Everything will be okay, stay here. I want to take a look at...the officer."

He stands up and walks toward Hugo's body. Multiple officers storm into the restroom, including Peter and Marcus.

Peter directly runs over to me. I start sobbing. "I'm sorry I couldn't do anything," I say. "I should've stood up for us."

Peter shakes his head and presses my head into his shoulder. "You did what you could. It's not your fault."

We both hear Marcus curse under his breath as he investigates the body.

"Do you need my help?" Peter asks him.

Marcus turns to him and angrily points his finger at him. "Get John out of here, now!"

Peter turns to me and gently grabs my arm. "Come on, let's leave the room," he tells me. "You'd feel better when you had some fresh air."

I nod, and he helps me up. I drop the tissue. Blood starts to drip onto the floor.

"Oh, fuck-" Peter curses. He takes some toilet paper and gently daps it on my nose before keeping it there. "Marcus! Do you have any tissues?"

Marcus groans. He doesn't seem very happy at the moment. He turns to us and curses even more. He takes out some tissues and gives them to Peter.

Peter gently takes away the toilet paper and replaces it with a tissue. He takes my arm and leads me out of the restroom.

We walk back to the office, where Anastasia waits for us.

"Oh, god!" Anastasia shouts as she sees us. She pulls a chair from under the table and lets me sit on it.

She grabs a tissue box and places it in front of me. I stare at it without moving a muscle. I can feel their worried gazes upon me.

"John?" Peter asks, shaking my arm slightly. I look at him and realize that blood is dripping onto my hoodie since I didn't change the tissue.

"Sorry," I apologize quietly. I take another tissue and replace the old one.

Anastasia comes and sits next to me. She gently rubs my back. "How do you feel, John?"

I shrug. "I don't know."

"I'll get you a cup of coffee," she says. She stands up and walks to the door.

"Make that a cup of tea!" Peter shouts. Anastasia turns around and looks at us.

"Lemon balm..." I mumble.

They both look at me. "Sorry, dear. I didn't quite get that," Anastasia says.

"Lemon balm tea," I repeat a bit louder.

She nods, a bit surprised. "We have a tea genius in the room. I'll get it for you, dear."

With that information, she leaves the room.

Peter helps me with my bloody nose by passing me tissues since I forget that.

"Want me to call Jackson?" he softly asks.

I shake my head as I refuse. There's a comfortable silence as he helps me. He's so kind and gentle.

I try not to lean into his touch or his warmth.

After a minute or five, Marcus comes into the room. He doesn't look happy. "How is everything going here?" he asks. "How's your nose?"

"John's doing fine, quiet, but fine," Peter answers for me.

Marcus nods. "And his nose?"

"Still bleeding. It's luckily not broken," Peter says. "Oh, that reminds me." He turns to me and takes another tissue. "Let's see how it is."

He slowly pulls away the tissue I'm holding. Blood starts dripping onto it. "Still bad," Peter says, changing the tissue.

"How bad is it?" Marcus asks.

"I don't know. It's just bleeding," Peter replies.

Marcus walks over to me and sits on the opposite side. "Talk to me, John," Marcus says. "What did you see?"

"Mr. Anderson, now?" Peter asks. I don't know why he used his last name.

"Yes, now," Marcus replies. "Maybe he saw something. I don't want him to forget things again."

I swallow and look down at my lap. I hear Peter sigh heavily. He rubs my back slowly. "Are you okay?" he asks me.

I force a smile and nod. Peter knows I'm lying. He lets me lean against him while he continues to stroke my back.

I see him glare at Marcus, who presses his lips together with a bit of guilt.

We stay quiet as the minutes pass by.

Anastasia comes back with the tea. As soon as I smell it, I stand up, well, tried to. As I stand up, my hood gets stuck between Peter's fingers. As I get loose, I stumble over my feet, which leads to me falling over another chair. I end up on the floor, not even near Anastasia.

I groan loudly. Anastasia kneels beside me and hands me a cup. "Tea?" she asks, raising her eyebrow, probably thinking if that would make me feel better.

I grab the cup from her hand and sit up, smiling slightly. I wipe away the blood from my nose and blow into a tissue for extra. The tissue ends up covered in blood. I throw it away as if it were nothing. I see Anastasia glaring weirdly at me.

I take a good sniff of the tea. The lemon, grassy, and minty smell fills my nose. I blow slightly before taking a sip. I take a deep breath and smile as the sweet liquid meets my tongue. I love savoring the first sip of a good cup of tea.

Anastasia chuckles, still looking confused. I lick my lips as I look at her with a questioning look.

"How much do you like tea?" she asks.

"Addiction!" Peter and Marcus say in sync. They've gotten closer to us.

Peter has the box of tissues with him. "He has a whole cabinet for his tea," Peter says. "He even knows what the perfect temperature is for the water!"

Anastasia starts to laugh. "I don't know if I should find that fascinating or scary. Will you make tea if I ever come to your place?"

"He would most likely do that," Marcus says. "He did it for Peter and I when we were there."

They all look at me as I make a noise whenever I sip the tea.

"What? It's hot!" I use it as an excuse.

Peter scoffs and says: "Why is there always something with you when it comes to hot liquids?"

I shrug and answer: "How am I supposed to know?"

"Oh, I don't know. Maybe because you are you?"

"Hush, Pudding!"

"Hush, Cheesecake!"

I stick out my tongue to him, and he does the same. Marcus groans while Anastasia chuckles. "You two are children," Marcus says.

We stay quiet as I finish my tea. We sit around the table. When I finish, everyone turns to Marcus. He's been clicking with a pen for the past few minutes.

"Alright, are we ready?" he asks.

Everyone nods.

"Good," Marcus says. "We'll be needing more people for this case."

"How about people who don't hate me?" Peter asks.

Anastasia nods. "That sounds like a good idea. No hate for Peter equals no more officers down."

"Okay, you have a point with that," Marcus agrees. He turns to me. "Are you able to answer questions?"

I nod in response. "Yes, sir."

"Alright," Marcus says. He takes out a notebook and keeps the pen open. "Did you see any faces?"

"No, he had his face covered with a mask."

He writes it down.

"Weapons?"

"Hands and the water. I didn't see everything because I panicked. I have a feeling he broke one of his bones. The sound echoed in the room."

Marcus writes it down. "Yes, his left forearm is broken. People?"

"Only him."

"Voice?"

"Husky as in very rough."

"Clothes?"

"Black."

"Skin or anything else shown?"

"Nothing."

"Did you see how he did it?"

"He asked before breaking Hugo's arm. He let Hugo gasp for air as he drowned him."

"What happened to you?"

"He came through the window. He pushed me against the wall and pinned me there. He told me to keep quiet, his voice breathy and smoky. He rubbed his thumb onto my lips as he covered my eyes. Then Hugo came, and you already know the rest."

"Tell us anyway."

"Okay, he hit Hugo in the face. He took off his necktie and turned back to me. He stuffed it inside my mouth. I was too afraid to fight back. He pushed me into the stall. I don't really know what happened next."

"How did you feel when you saw the body?"

"Nothing."

Marcus stops writing and looks up at me. "What?"

"I felt nothing," I repeat. I look down at the cup that's on my lap. "Nothing is all I felt."

I realize what I want to do with Peter. I want to pin him against the wall, touch his lips, and make him mine.

"It's a dead body. Not the first I have seen," I say. I shrug. "I didn't feel a thing."

Anastasia clears her throat. "John, it's nothing to worry about. You don't need to hide your feelings."

I shake my head and look up at her. "I'm not hiding, Anastasia. I'm being serious. I felt nothing," I tell her. I look at Marcus. He seems as surprised as Anastasia. "It was scary in the beginning, but then it felt like nothing."

"I'm getting you a therapist," Marcus says.

"No need," I reply. "I'm completely fine."

Peter stands up, walks toward me, and forces me to look at him. "Tell me something."

"I'm fine."

He shakes his head. "No. My friend would never say that."

I chuckle slightly. "I. Felt. Nothing. I've seen death before. I guess I got used to it."

Marcus gets up and dials a number on his phone. Someone picks up. "I want to make an appointment for a victim of a murder."

CHAPTER 14

Anastasia walks me home. Marcus wanted to discuss this with Peter. We arrive at the doorstep. Anastasia and I both look up at the door.

"I really didn't feel a thing," I tell her softly. "Is there something wrong with me?"

She sighs and smiles slightly. "It's probably nothing," she tells me. "It's just surprising that you felt nothing."

I nod. The door opens. My jaw drops as I see the person standing there. Her hair brown just like mine, her eyes hazel brown like my father's, and her smile as wide as ever. "Johny!" she shouts.

"Juliette?" I ask, still surprised.

She spreads her arms and runs over to me. We give each other a big hug. She lets go and looks at Anastasia.

"Hey there!" she says. "I'm Juliette Welling!"

Anastasia's jaw also drops. Her eyes widen as she forms a smile. "You're his sister?" she asks.

"Yes, I am!" Juliette says, pointing at herself. "Are you his girlfriend?"

"Juliette!" I shout. "I'm bisexual!"

She falls quiet and looks at me. "Sorry, what?"

I pat her shoulder, pressing my lips together after realizing what I just shouted. I slip beside her and walk toward the door, lifting my shoulders in embarrassment.

As soon as I see the person standing by the doorframe, I drop them. I smile at him. He has his hair in a messy man bun, and his eyes shine as he sees me. "¡Hola, hermano!" he says.

"José!" I say.

We walk toward each other and give each other a big hug.

He pats my back, pulls away, and has a good look at me from top to toe. "You're as skinny as ever," he says with the most Spanish accent. It makes me chuckle.

"Shut up, big bear!" I hiss back at him.

He laughs.

"What are you two doing here?" I ask him.

"Well, we thought that a visit wouldn't hurt!" he answers.

I nod and give him a playful push on the shoulder. "Well, you're absolutely right. I missed you, bro."

He smiles widely and gives me another hug.

Jackson's head pops out from the bathroom. "Hi!" he greets me.

I wave at him. "Sup!"

I turn around. Juliette stands behind me. "You're bisexual?" she shouts as loud as possible, her face only a few inches away from mine.

"Yes! Yes, I am!" I shout back at her.

José grabs my shoulder and then me around. "¿Tú qué? (You're what?)" he asks me.

I chuckle shyly and nod. "I fell in love with a cop."

"What do you mean? ¿Qué pasó con Lily? (What happened with Lily?)" he asks me.

"Ella me engañó. (She cheated on me.)" I tell them.

His eyes widen slightly. "She what? Oh, hermano..." He hugs me again. Juliette joins the hug.

There's a car heard in front. We turn to it. Marcus and Peter step out. Anastasia greeted them as they stepped out.

I grab my siblings' ears and whisper: "I have a crush on Peter."

I let go of them. I walk toward Peter and Marcus as if nothing happened. "Hey!" I greet them. "What are you doing here?"

"Oh, just seeing how everything's going," Peter says.

Marcus clears his throat, causing me to look at him. "No, we're here because Peter kept begging me."

I can't help but burst out in laughter. Anastasia starts to laugh too. Peter groans and covers his face with his hands.

"Who are they?" Marcus suddenly asks. We all look at him and follow his gaze.

I look at Peter and pat his shoulder. "They're my siblings!" I tell them.

Peter's eyes widen. He looks at me with his mouth wide open. He points at José. My brother waves. "That's your brother?" Peter asks. "Your Spanish brother?"

I nod. "I only have one brother and one sister."

Peter grabs my shoulders and shakes me up. I get dizzy and almost fall onto him. "Peter!" I shout.

He stops shaking me. I try stepping back but stumble over my feet, causing me to fall onto him. We both fall onto the ground, me on top of him.

I groan as I open my eyes. "Ouch..."

My breath hitches as I realize that I'm lying on Peter. He looks me in the eyes. I'm not sure if I'm imagining it, but I see his cheeks have a light pink color.

In embarrassment, I get up as quickly as possible and run toward José and Juliette, shouting: "¡Ayudadme! (Help me!)"

They both start to laugh. I hide behind José. I see Peter get up and wipe off the dust.

Marcus and Anastasia look surprised at us. They didn't know I could speak Spanish.

José grabs me and pushes me back out there. Juliette has to lean against the doorframe as she laughs. "¡Te odio! (I hate you!)" I shout at them.

Peter chuckles slightly behind me. I turn to him. "S-sorry about that," I apologize.

He nods and puts his thumbs up. "All good."

We stay awkwardly silent for a bit. José clears his throat. We both look at him. He holds out his hand to Peter. "You must be Pedro," he says with a smile.

"That's your name in Spanish," I whisper to Peter.

He nods and smiles. He shakes his hand. "Pleasure meeting you," Peter says.

"Oh, please. The pleasure is mine. I'm José," José says.

They let go of each other. Peter looks at Juliette. She waves at him. "¡Hola! I'm Juliette!"

"Hola, ¿cómo estás? (Hello, how are you?)" Peter replies.

I nearly choked on air. "The fuck did you just say?" I ask him.

Peter chuckles slightly and scratches his neck. "I asked my father what he knew in Spanish. That was his response."

"Sounds like a lovely dad!" Juliette says. "Are you single?"

Why is it always a pain to be the youngest? Why did she need to ask that?

"Yes, I am single," Peter awkwardly answers.

"Hey!" Anastasia shouts from behind us. "Are we allowed in this conversation or not?"

I gesture to the door. "Anyone tea? I'll make tea!"

I quickly step inside and rush to the kitchen, cursing under my breath. I sigh and get out the things needed for the tea.

I turn on the stove and put on a pot of water. After that, I started making little bags.

I hear the door close but don't turn around.

They talk amongst each other. They laugh with each other.

I spoon a teaspoon of dried peppermint leaves into the bags and close them. As the water reaches the right temperature, Peter comes over.

"Hey, Cheesecake," he says.

I chuckle slightly before replying: "Hey, Pudding." I gesture to the bags and the pot. "Be gentle."

With a smile, Peter takes the bags and slowly places them into the boiling water.

I take the mugs and spoons as he does. I just realized that everyone went quiet.

Peter watches me as I focus on the tea. I stir the water slightly before taking out the bags. I pour the tea into the mugs. I put them on a template with a cup of honey in the middle.

"You're addicted," Peter whispers.

I chuckle slightly and wink at him. I take the template and join the rest. I place it in the middle of the table and sit on the floor since there is no more space on the couch. Peter sits next to me.

Everyone takes a mug.

"Geez, this smells better than the tea I made," Anastasia says.

Her comment makes me smile.

I add a quarter of my spoon of honey to my tea. I stir it slightly and take on the fresh smell. Someone chuckles.

Looking confused, I look at Juliette. "You always love the first sip of your tea," she tells me. "I remember how you got into it!"

José starts to chuckle too. "Oh, yes. It's actually a lovely story."

Peter snaps his finger and points at them. "Tell us!" he asks.

"Oh, no!" I say. I start feeling embarrassed as I remember everything. "I just want to have my tea!"

They all begin to laugh.

"He was eight when he first got into tea," José begins. "We drank tea with our grandparents. He took a sip and made a weird face."

Juliette giggles and continues. "He said he didn't like it. Guess what he did three days later?"

"What did he do?" Jackson asks.

"That night, I went downstairs because it started to smell. It did smell nice," José answers. "I found John in the kitchen with a flashlight and a book. He was legit making tea on his own!"

"No, he did not!" Peter says. He turns to me and gives me a playful push. "You never said you were a cutie as a child! You're adorable now but as a child? Do you have pictures?"

I groan and cover my face with my hands. "Shut up!" I shout, embarrassed. "Why can't I just get my tea?"

"Come on, hermano! You were adorable when you were doing that!" José says.

Marcus claps his hands. "That's what I wanted to ask! Why didn't you tell us you speak Spanish?"

I shrug with my lips pressed together. "I don't know. Maybe because I never knew there was a moment to." I look at Peter. "You found out today this morning!"

"And I found out just now!" Jackson shouts. "Bro! We've been friends for so many years!"

I chuckle softly. "Yeah, sorry about that. Wait, you already knew my brother! How did you not recognize his heavy accent?"

My brother clears his throat. "¿Cómo te atreves? (How dare you?) I speak fluently English!"

"In your dreams!" I tease him.

José turns to Juliette. "Soy bueno en inglés, ¿verdad? (I'm good at English, right?)" he asks.

My sister clicks her tongue, shaking her head. "You have a massive accent."

José gasps. He hits the left side of his chest as if he's just been struck by an arrow. He starts saying words in Spanish about how he's good in English.

Everyone looks confused at him while Juliette can't stop laughing.

I roll my eyes with a smile and turn back to my tea, which has cooled down. I shut my eyes and try to lock out all the noise. I like to drink my tea quietly.

The sounds fade away after a second or five. I take a deep breath before drinking my tea. The minty liquid meets my tongue, which makes me smile. I feel my shoulders drop as I relax completely.

Suddenly, I hear a faint sound. I open my eyes and look at Peter. Confused, I blink a couple of times. He chuckles. "You really zone out when it comes to tea," he tells me.

I feel my cheeks flush from shame. "I-I'm sorry," I stutter. "Did anyone say something?"

Peter shakes his head. "No, we were just looking at you."

"Not in the wrong way, of course!" Juliette says. "We don't want any boys having boners!"

My jaw drops at her comment. Jackson starts laughing, nearly falling off the couch. Anastasia's eyes widen as she looks down at her tea. It starts to get awkward.

I change my position and take another big sip of my drink.

"Okay, so, Peter. How many times have you dated someone?" Juliette suddenly asks.

My breath hitches at her question. "¡Hermana!" I shout. "Have manners!"

"Says the bitch who zones out every three minutes!" she hisses back with a smirk.

"¡Ya está! ¡Me voy! (That's it! I'm going!)" I say, putting my hands up. I take my cup and walk to the kitchen.

Everyone falls quiet. I finish drinking and place the cup in the sink. I go to the door, put on my shoes and jacket, and take the keys.

"¡Hermano, lo siento! (Brother, I'm sorry!)" my sister apologizes.

I ignore her, open the door, and slam it shut. I sigh deeply and continue walking. I hear the door open.

"John!" José shouts. I don't turn around or do anything in response.

They don't run after me, except for one person, Peter. "John! Wait up!" he shouts after me.

I can't help but listen to him. I want to be with him so badly. I turn around.

Peter pants as he catches his breath. "Oh, Jesus Christ! You're fast."

I chuckle slightly. "Sorry," I say. "And sorry about earlier. It's hard being the youngest."

He smiles widely at me. "You're the youngest? I thought Juliette was the youngest."

I shake my head. "Guessed wrong."

We stay quiet for a moment and look at each other.

Peter runs a hand through his hair as his breathing becomes normal.

I watch as his fingers brush his hair, the muscles in his arms move, and how the fabric of his clothing folds and creases with his movements.

The sun starts to shine again. I watch as the light hits Peter's face. It looks magnificent. The way the color of his eyes gets more visible.

I see a smile tug at the corner of his lips. He looks at me and asks in the sweetest voice: "Are you okay?"

With that question, I get dragged back into reality. I clear my throat and start fidgeting with my hands. "Y-yes!" I stutter. "Perfectly fine! Okie-dokie! Tickety-boo!"

Peter falls quiet for a moment but chuckles right after. "You're adorable," he says.

He runs a hand through my hair and lets it rest on the back of my head. We look each other in the eyes.

God, give me strength. I try as hard as possible to not lean into his touch. I want him so badly.

"Are you alright?" he asks me.

I press my lips together and nod slightly. Peter holds his head to one side and asks: "Are you sure?"

I nod again.

"Would you like some coffee?" he asks.

"Maybe something stronger?" I ask. "I could use some alcohol right now."

Peter scoffs and quietly laughs. "I didn't expect you to be a drinker."

I shrug. "From time to time."

"Interesting," Peter says. "But alright, we can go to the bar."

CHaPTer 15

Peter and I walk to the bar together. He mostly does the talking since I love listening to his voice.

We arrive at the bar and stop at the entrance. Peter looks at me. "Are you sure?"

I nod with a smile. "Yes, I'm sure. What could go wrong? We have each other."

Peter smiles back at me. We enter the building. The smell of alcohol fills our noses.

We take seats at the counter.

"So, what kind of alcohol do you drink?" Peter asks me. He smirks slightly.

I grin and tap the counter two times. A bartender comes and asks: "What can I get you?"

"A glass of vodka, please," I tell him.

The bartender gets out a glass and looks at Peter. "What about you?"

"A glass of whiskey, perhaps?" he says.

The man nods and fills one glass with vodka and the other with whiskey. He puts some ice in both and a lime slice in Peter's drink.

"I did not expect that from you," Peter tells me, chuckling slightly and playing with his lime.

I shrug with a grin. "Well, I don't drink that much, so whenever I do, I drink a lot."

Peter pats my shoulder. "Respect, man, respect."

I laugh slightly and take a sip of my drink. I lick my lips wet and smile. "Ooh, that's some good vodka."

Peter laughs. He takes a sip of his drink and sticks out his tongue. It makes me chuckle.

He looks at me and points at my drink. I get the cue. We both grab our glasses, and he starts counting.

"Ready? One, two, three!"

We both gulped down our drinks. We both laugh as Peter almost chokes on his drink.

"Now, my question is, how quickly do you sober up?" I ask Peter.

"In a minute or ten, it depends on how much I've drunk," Peter replies.

I grin as an idea pops up in my head. "Try vodka."

Peter chuckles slightly. "You're kidding, right?"

I shake my head and call the bartender again. "Two glasses of vodka, please."

Peter starts laughing. "Oh, no. I'm going to die!"

I laugh and pat his shoulder. "It's just a drink!"

"Fine! Fine!" he says, taking the glass. I take mine.

I see Peter hesitate. He looks at me, and I nod. He sighs and chuckles slightly.

He takes a deep breath before finally gulping down the drink in one go. Peter coughs slightly.

He groans slightly and shakes his head. "Oh, geez... How do you manage to do this?"

I grin and pass him my glass. Peter shakes his head. "I'm already feeling tipsy. I'll get drunk with that one."

"Come on, one more drink," I tell him. "I can get two for me."

Peter sighs and takes the glass. "Alright."

He starts drinking. I put some money on the counter. I take Peter's arm and help him up.

I help him outside. I stopped a taxi. We both get in, Peter almost tripping over his feet. I tell the driver Peter's address, and we get going.

Peter looks tired during the ride.

When we get to his house, I pay the driver and help Peter out. I keep him on his feet as we walk toward the door. I take his keys and open the door.

I help him to his room and place him on the bed. He's sweating and breathing rapidly.

I take off my jacket and hoodie.

I take out my gloves and turn back to Peter. He looks confused at me.

"John? What are you doing?" he asks. He chuckles slightly and rubs his eyes.

I smile slightly at him. I grab his chin and force him to look up at me. "Do you happen to have a camera?"

Peter looks at one of the drawers. I walk over to the drawers. I found a video camera in the first drawer. Next to it, there's another camera. I take both.

I turn back to Peter with the video camera and place it on the nightstand. I push his back onto the bed and sit on his waist. He looks up at me but doesn't do anything.

"Do you know how crazy you drive me?" I ask him. I grab his neck, my eyes still locked in his. "Do you know what I crave?"

"What the fuck are you doing?" Peter asks me, grabbing my wrist. He doesn't push me away yet. A smile tugs at the corner of his lips. "Are you going to fuck me?"

I grunt slightly. "You drive me mad!" I snarl at him. I tighten my grip around his neck. "Goodness, making you drunk was the best idea so far."

Peter softly coughs. I lick my lips. "Nah, not today. As tempting as it is, I won't do it."

I grab him by his hair, lift him, and push him onto his pillows. I take one of his ties out of the drawer. I feel Peter's gaze upon me. He doesn't seem to mind it. How drunk is he?

I take his wrists and hold them above his head. I see his legs kick. I tie his wrists together with the necktie. "Keep your hands there."

"What if I don't?" Peter asks, his tone sounding more concerned now.

I lick my lips and grab the tie. "Nevermind, I'll just tie you to it."

I tie his wrists to the headboard. I look down at him as I do it. I see anger in his eyes but also fear. "Don't be afraid, Pudding. Everything will be just fine."

Looking at his body, I think about what I could do to him. I sit on his waist again.

I tug the hem of his shirt. Peter tries to break free and starts kicking. I grin. "Relax, my love," I say softly. "This won't hurt."

I take it, pull it up to his eyes, and blindfold him with it.

My hands slide over his chest. I take in his scent. I gently caress his shoulders as I do.

Peter starts kicking again. "Stop!" he shouts as if I would listen.

I grin and let my hands slide over his chest. I let my thumbs rub his nipples in circular motions.

"Fuck..." I mumble. I let go of his body. "D-do you want me to stop?"

"Yes!" he shouts as loud as possible.

I arch my back and let go of his body. "I don't know what came over me."

As much as I don't want to cause him discomfort, I feel something hard by my rear, which draws my attention.

"You want me to stop, yet you still get hard," I mumble. "How do you expect me to stop?"

I reach for the waist of his pants. His belt annoyed me anyway. I take it off and pull down his pants. I can't help but bite my lip as I see the bulge in his underwear.

Peter told me to stop, yet, he doesn't fight back now. I can hear him whimper softly.

"Tell me, do you want me to pleasure you?" I ask.

He doesn't answer with words. He shakes his head. But his body betrays him. His hips buckle as I slide my hand over his penis.

He wants me to stop. I want to stop for him. But my body doesn't let me.

I know I can't leave any trails of saliva behind, so I'll have to use my hands.

I pull down his underwear. It's so hard and quite big. My first reaction was to touch it. Peter squirmed as I did. I let go.

I take the camera and get off him. I take a few steps back and take multiple pictures of him.

Seeing him tied down, naked, and hard arouses me. I start cupping my own erection.

I place down the camera and walk back over to the bed. I take out the pictures and start shaking it until it's visible. I place them both on the nightstand.

I spread his legs and sit between them. I start stroking his penis.

Looking at his hands, I realize that they are clenched into fists.

"S-stop!" he whimpers. "Please, Whoever you are!"

With that last sentence, I look at him. I deepen my voice and ask: "You don't know me?"

"No, I don't!" Peter shouts.

It seems like he's sober now. "Does your head hurt?"

Peter tries to break free. I keep him down by punching his ribs. He gasps and coughs

"Don't be naughty. Bad boys get punished," I tell him.

I close my hand around his erection and slowly move it up and down. Peter squirms under my touch. I go faster, watching him squirm, and try to keep his mouth shut.

As I focus on his cock, I suddenly hear a noise, causing me to stop. It seems like Peter has been keeping moans for himself.

I look back at his cock and go faster. I don't care anymore. I continue to jerk him off. He groans and arches his back. I lick my lips and get the recorder. I started filming.

"Come on..." I softly say, my voice a bit smokier. "Come on, let go."

Peter's face seems flushed, his teeth grit and his hands clench tightly.

I look back down at his rear. With my other hand, I go down to his behind. My finger swirls around his anal. I want him to come.

I push a finger inside him, causing him to gasp. His lips part, and he groans.

I continue to jerk him off and slide another finger into his ass. Finally, he lets out a loud moan. I start fingering him as he squirms.

"S-stop!" he begs me. "P-please!"

I can't stop. I know what I want, and I will get it, whatever it takes.

He throws his head back and presses his lips together. I can hear him moan inside his mouth as he finally climaxes.

Peter starts panting. I let go of him. I turn off the recorder.

I get off him and step away. I take the camera and take multiple pictures of him. I lick off his semen from my gloves.

I take my clothes, put on my hood, and cover my face. I untied his hands and then let down his shirt.

His eyes directly focus on me. He seems angry but too weak to do anything. I leave one of the pictures on the nightstand and leave the recorder on the bed.

"You taste amazing, Peter," I say, still in a mysterious voice. "I can't wait to do the same with John."

Peter tries to get up but falls to the ground as he tries to. "Don't you fucking touch him!"

I shake my head and take my leave. Peter follows me downstairs. Well, he falls down the stairs.

I look at him. "Well, that's something you don't see every day."

"Don't touch him!" he shouts.

"Spare your breath, darling," I tell him. "You'll need it when you want to scream the next time you see me."

I turn to the door and go outside. Three minutes later, my phone started to ring. It's Peter.

"Hey, Peter! How are you doing?" I ask. "You were pretty drunk earlier, so I brought you home."

He breathes heavily into the phone. "You need to hide, John! Get to Marcus!" he says between breaths.

"Woah, Peter! Why are you so out of breath?" I ask him, trying to sound as innocent as possible.

"He's coming for you! The murderer is coming for you!" he warns me. "Get to Marcus as soon as possible!"

I start breathing quickly for the effect. "What? W-what about you?" I ask, stuttering. "A-are you okay?"

"Get to Marcus! Don't worry about me!"

I hang up and start running back to Jackson's place. I take off my gloves and hide them in my pockets.

CHAPTER 16

I start banging on the door as I arrive. Marcus opens it. I let myself fall into him, panting heavily.

"Woah, John!" he says. "Are you okay? What happened?"

He wraps his arms around me, trying to comfort me.

"P-Peter! H-he-" I keep stuttering and start pacing around the room. "Peter..."

"What about him?" Anastasia asks.

I run a trembling hand through my hair.

"He called me, telling me that the murderer was coming after me," I tell them. "I think he just got to Peter!"

Marcus curses under his breath again. He grabs his phone and starts dialing a number. He runs outside to the car. Anastasia wants to follow, but Marcus orders her to stay with us.

My siblings help me to the couch.

"¿Qué está pasando? (What's going on?)" Juliette asks me.

"There has been a murderer, a stalker, running around town," Anastasia explains. "He's obsessed with Peter and John."

"How did you just-?" Jackson asks.

"Guessed it."

Anastasia kneels in front of me. She holds her hand on my forehead. "How do you feel?"

I shake my head, keeping my mouth shut. José puts his arm around me.

"Since when did this all start?" Juliette asks with a slight accent. She runs a hand through my hair.

Anastasia looks at Juliette, then at José, and lastly at me. "The first murder happened about a week and a half ago. Your brother was a victim."

José's grip on my shoulder tightens. "What?" He turns to me. "¿Por qué no dijiste nada? (Why didn't you say something?) You could've called!"

"José! He's stressed!" my sister argues. "Be nice!"

"I am being nice, hermanita!" José shouts.

They keep shouting at each other. I cover my ear while whispering under my breath: "Stop it."

Everyone keeps arguing with me in the middle. I hear voices, but they're not theirs.

"You're invisible," the voices tell me. "Show them that you exist!"

"If you don't do anything, then what are you worth?"

"Maybe it's better if they hate you!"

"QUIET!" I shout from the top of my lungs. "EVERYONE, SHUT THE FUCK UP!"

Everyone falls quiet. The voices are gone too.

I get up and lock myself up in the bathroom.

"Hermano!" José shouts. "Please, open the door." He gently knocks on the door. "I'm sorry about earlier."

"Vete, por favor. (Go away, please.)" I whisper.

My phone starts ringing. I don't want to pick up or even look who it is.

I walk toward the sink and get out my gloves. I hold them by my nose and take a deep breath.

His scent is still on them.

I remember Jackson having plastic bags in the top cabinets. I take one of them and place the gloves in it.

"I'm going to need new gloves..." I whisper. I look up at the ceiling. "Hmm..."

I stand on the toilet seat and hit one of the ceiling plates. It's loose. I remove one plate and hide the bag in the ceiling. I place the plate bag and get off the toilet.

My phone rings again. I ignore it again.

"John! Open the door!" Jackson shouts. I ignore him.

I look at myself in the mirror. "Goodness...what have I become?"

I turn on the water and let the sink fill.

Their knocks on the door become louder.

I get out the first aid kit. I open it and get out a knife.

Taking a deep breath, I hold the knife by my bruise. I press it harder against my skin. It cuts into my flesh.

The pain doesn't bother me at all. It starts to bleed. The blood drips into the water.

I take a small cotton ball and dap it on the wound. I look in the mirror into my eyes. I start outlining my body with the blood. I squeeze the cut or make another one for more blood.

I draw horns and a tail on the outlining. Above my head, I write: Devil in disguise

The door burst open. I turn to it and hide my hands behind my back as quickly as possible.

It's Marcus. "You really need to pick up the phone, John."

I guess a lot more time has passed by than I thought.

He looks at the mirror and back at me. "Show me your hands."

I shake my head as I refuse.

Behind him, I see the rest. They look at the mirror. Juliette holds José's hand while covering her mouth in shock.

Marcus steps toward me, and I step back. We look each other in the eyes. He reaches a hand toward me. "I'm here to help," he tells me soothingly. "Trust me, John."

I keep stepping back until I reach the wall. I let a tear roll down my face. "I'm sorry," I whisper. "For being such a worthless piece of shit."

Marcus shakes his head. "Everything is okay. You're not worthless or useless. You're a good guy."

"You don't know that!" I shout. "What if I say that I did bad things? Horrible things?"

"I'll listen," he says. "We'll get through it together. Peter will be there too and Anastasia too. If you want your siblings, then that's fine too."

"I just want silence," I whisper. "Everything is so loud."

"How loud?" he asks me.

I shake my head. I hold up my hands. I drop the knife and cotton balls. "Don't be mad..."

Marcus slowly approaches me. "It's okay," he continuously whispers.

When he's only a few steps away from me, he takes my hands. He still looks me in the eyes. "Let's take care of this, okay? We'll take care of you."

Marcus steps back, and I follow. He stops at the sink. He opens the first aid kit and gets out the antiseptic. Marcus looks at Anastasia.

She walks into the room and stands on the other side. She smiles reassuringly at me. Anastasia puts a finger in the water.

"How about we clean your wounds first?" she asks me. "The water has a good temperature."

I nod. She gently takes my hands and places them in the water. It stings slightly.

Marcus takes off his jacket.

He uses the sleeve to pick up the knife.

Anastasia lifts my hands and takes the antiseptic. She pours it on some cotton balls and holds it over my wounds. "This can hurt a bit. Are you ready?" she asks me. I nod in response.

She smiles and gently daps the cotton balls onto my wounds. She was right. It does hurt slightly.

Marcus walks to the door and sends everyone to the living room, including my siblings.

"Peter?" I hear someone shout, questioning.

I turn my head to the door. Marcus closes it and walks toward me to help Anastasia with my wounds.

"Was that- Is Peter here?" I ask Marcus.

He pats my shoulder reassuringly. "Yes, that was him. He's doing alright, no need to worry."

"Can we see him?" I ask.

"Soon, dear. But first, we need to take care of your wounds," Anastasia tells me.

I sigh and look into the mirror. I see something else.

I see the room bloody. I am in the center. Behind me, there are the people I have murdered. Their wounds are visible, but I don't feel disgusted.

The voices in my head come back.

"Why did you murder us?" Hugo's voice asks. "I thought we were friends."

"Peter was my friend. You hurt him!" Iliana shouts.

"Why did you do it?" George asks. "You are a selfish monster!"

They all reach out to me. I flinch. I pull my hands away and step back quickly.

Marcus grabs my shoulders, helping me from tumbling over. "Calm down, John," he says. "We're here. You're safe. We're all safe."

I look around. My breathing is ragged. There's no blood anymore. The dead aren't here anymore.

Marcus cups my face, making me look at him. "You're safe. Everything is okay. What did you see?"

I stay still for a moment, trying to calm down. Anastasia and Marcus both wait patiently for me.

"The dead... The dead were here," I whisper, my voice shaky. "The room was covered by blood."

"Everything is okay now," Anastasia soothingly tells me. "Would you like to go to the rest?"

I nod in response. Marcus lets me go. The two lead me to the living room.

Everyone stands up to look at me. My gaze directly falls on Peter.

Marcus and Anastasia help me to the couch. José and Juliette sit next to each other next to me so Peter could sit on the other side.

Peter takes my hand and gently squeezes it. "Are you alright?" he asks me softly.

I nod, not wanting to say a thing. But I force myself for Peter. "H-how are you?"

"Oh, John..." Peter pulls me close and hugs me tightly.

"I'm so sorry..." I whisper to Peter. "This is all my fault."

Peter shakes his head. "No, this isn't. Everything is alright."

I pull away and look him in the eyes. "This is all my fault."

"No, stop blaming yourself!" Peter says. "It's not your fault!"

"It is!" I shout back. "It is! It is! It is! I'm going mad!"

"You're not! Believe me. You're not going mad!"

"Yes, I am!"

"No! Believe in yourself!"

"Why won't you just fucking believe me?"

"Because we all know that isn't true!"

I grab a cushion and hit Peter with it.

He looks surprised at me. "What was that for?" he asks, confused with a hint of anger.

"My whole life is messed up!" I shout. "The moment you stepped into my life!"

"What do you mean?" Peter asks.

"Never mind. You wouldn't get it!"

I get up and walk toward the door. I leave the house and sit on the doorstep. I sigh deeply. "Fuck..."

I hear footsteps approach me.

"Hermano?" It's Juliette.

She sits next to me and leans against my shoulder. I place a kiss on her temple. I let my head rest against hers. "Are you alright?" she asks me.

"Can we just...not talk about it right now?" I ask her pleadingly. "I don't want to think about it."

I see her smile slightly. "Of course, brother."

We stay quiet like this. It feels so much better to have someone to lean on. Everyone needs a moment of silence with the person they love once in a while.

I take her hand and squeeze it gently. "I have a huge secret that keeps pulling me down. Can you keep such a secret?"

My sister looks at me. "I'll try."

I shake my head. "I can't tell you if you try. I need you to be sure you can keep it."

She nods and holds out her pink. "Pinky promise."

I smile slightly and let our pinks intertwine.

I get closer to her ear. "I'm the murderer."

I hear her breath hitch. She freezes. "It's been a burden for a while. I don't know what to do anymore."

She looks at me. "You have to tell Marcus," she whispers back.

I shake my head. "I'm afraid of what will happen."

"What did you do to Peter?" she asks me.

"I..." I look down at my hands. They're trembling. "I couldn't stop it. Please, believe me. I couldn't stop it!"

"What did you do?" she asks me again.

I look at the door. Everyone watches us. I fall quiet and look down at my trembling hands. "I should've stabbed myself when I had the chance..."

"John!" Juliette shouts. "Don't ever say that again!"

I hear them whisper amongst each other. Marcus goes back inside.

I look at the police car. Juliette follows my gaze. "No! Don't you even dare!" she shouts. She grabs my arm. "Don't!"

I pull my arm away and walk toward the car. I open the door. Peter and José run toward me.

There's a gun lying on the car floor. I try taking it. Peter and my brother try pulling me away.

"John! Think straight!" Peter shouts. "Everything will be okay!"

I manage to grab the gun. José tries to hit the gun out of my hands but fails.

"John!" my sister cries out pleadingly.

"I'm sorry," I say softly.

Peter tries pulling my hand with the gun away from my head. I pull the trigger.

CHAPTER 17

Nothing happens.

We all look at it. Peter sighs heavily in relief. I see my brother's eyes filled with tears.

"It isn't loaded..." José mumbles, relieved.

"Drop the gun, John," Peter tells me.

I drop the gun and sink to my knees. I feel my eyes start to water. I sniff softly and start sobbing.

José kneels beside me and hugs me tightly. Marcus comes over. He holds up a syringe. "This is a light sedative. You'll feel a bit better with it. We're going to take care of you, okay?"

I nod. I take a deep breath as Marcus injects me with the sedative.

I lean against José.

"Brother?" I ask softly. "Do you think I'm insane?"

"No," he tells me, kissing my forehead. "Of course not."

I close my eyes and nuzzle into his neck, falling asleep slowly.

I open my eyes. I'm on my mattress. My head hurts slightly. I stay in bed for a bit longer, not wanting to get up yet.

My eyes fall shut again, but I don't fall asleep.

The smell of chicken soup fills the room. I open my eyes and turn to my other side. José sits on the floor next to the bed. I see something in his hands. It makes me smile.

He turns to me. "John," he says. He sits on the edge of the mattress. He gently strokes a lock of hair from my face. "How do you feel?"

Juliette comes over. She sits next to José with a bowl of soup. I try to smile at both of them.

They help me sit up. Juliette hasn't said a thing yet. I'm not that surprised. I told her about the killing.

She holds the spoon with soup to my mouth. I open my mouth, and she feeds me. The liquid meets my tongue. It's hot, but I don't mind it.

I look around. Everyone's here. Alexander, Jasmine, Jackson, Marcus, Anastasia, Juliette, and José. The only person not here is Peter.

They gather around the mattress. I smile slightly. "Hey," I say, almost whispering.

I see Jasmine smile and hold Alexander's hand, which makes me smile wider.

The door opens. Peter comes in soaking wet. We all turn to him, and he starts coughing. "Next time, give me an umbrella!"

He walks toward the kitchen but stops when he sees me. He has bags with him. The bags have logos. He went to the supermarket and the pharmacy.

I wave at him. "Hey, Pudding," I say. I want to say something else, but Juliette shoves a spoon of soup into my mouth.

"Eat," she says. "You need your energy."

I swallow it and sigh. I reach out for the bowl, but my sister pulls it away. "No, ahorra fuerzas. (No, save your strength.)"

"Come on, I can-"

"No!"

We look each other in the eyes.

She looks mad.

I sign and get up. I hold on to a counter for support, trembling slightly. José tries helping me, but I refuse.

I wall to the front door. Marcus tries to stop me. "John! How about we talk?"

"Let me be, Marcus," I tell him. "I'll be fine."

"You tried to commit suicide. I don't think I can let you go on the streets like that."

"I don't care."

"John!" Peter shouts. "Coffee?"

I turn to him. He steps toward me. "Come on, let's get some coffee," he says.

He takes an umbrella and opens the door. I look at Marcus. He doesn't look like he knows what's happening. I shrug and follow Peter.

The two of us walk together under the umbrella in the rain.

Our arms brush against each other as we walk. We stay quiet and listen to the raindrops as they hit the ground. The cold breeze is comforting.

We got to the café. We both get in, still not saying a word.

Peter shuts the umbrella and places it in a holder. We wait together in line. I feel his hand brush against mine. I want to take it but don't do it.

It's our turn.

"What can I get you two gentlemen?" the cashier asks us.

"A decaf and an espresso, please," Peter orders.

The cashier nods with a smile and gets our order.

I keep my gaze on Peter. He looks at me with a comforting smile.

He takes our coffee and leads me to a table by the window.

He quietly places the decaf in front of me. I smile at him and take the cup. We both look outside.

I decided to break the silence between us. "Quite the weather, don't you think?"

I see Peter smile in our reflection. "Yeah, quite the weather."

"I could watch the raindrops hit the window for hours," I tell Peter. "The way the rain hits the ground or the umbrellas... It's just fascinating. People might hate it and want to run inside, but it's just nature."

I shut my mouth and smile slightly, thinking I am talking too much.

"Don't stop," Peter suddenly says. I turn to him. "I like hearing your voice."

I smile and look back outside, feeling a bit better.

Why do I want him so badly? Why do I need him so badly?

"Did you know that raindrops aren't actually tear-shaped? They're oval-shaped," I tell him. "They also have a smell."

I look at my coffee and blow before taking a small sip of it. Peter watches my every move.

I look up at him in suspicion. "Did Marcus set you up for this?"

Peter shakes his head, chuckling slightly. "No, no. He didn't," he tells me. "I just thought this would be a good idea. Plus, it's the daily routine, isn't it?"

Smiling at him, I nod once. "Good point, Pudding."

"Always am right, Cheesecake."

He raises his cup. I raise my cup in response.

We both look outside again. We watch the raindrops fall from the sky and hit the window. Cars pass by, wanting to go home. People run to cover. We watch as the drops slide down the glass.

I don't know if it's real, but I think I see Peter glance at me every few seconds.

He glances at me, and I turn to him. Peter's eyes widen slightly, and he looks away. I see his cheeks flush slightly.

"You look cute when you're flushed."

Peter looks at me. We look at each other for a minute before breaking eye contact.

"Sorry," I apologize. "That kind of slipped out..."

"You look cute too..." Peter whispers.

I bite my bottom lip with a slight smile.

I look back at the window. I see the reflection of a couple of people behind us. They're looking at Peter from time to time.

My smile immediately fades as I see it.

Clearing my throat, I get Peter's attention.

"What's wrong?" he asks me.

"People are watching you behind us," I tell him. "Look at the reflections."

Peter does as I told him. He clears his throat and takes a sip of his coffee. "I recognize them. Old 'friends'."

"Huh?"

"Class bullies. Nothing to worry about."

"Why don't we go say hi? They might have changed?"

Peter sighs. "Fine." He gets up and winks at me. "If it sucks, it's your fault."

It makes me chuckle. I get up. We both turn to Peter's old 'friends' and walk toward them.

"Hello, Eric, Lucas, and Henry," Peter awkwardly says.

Eric looks like a white polar bear. He has white hair and brown eyes. He seems nice.

Lucas, on the other hand, looks like a grizzly. His hair is a huge mess, and he has a short beard. His eyes have a deep brown color.

Henry looks like a spoiled boy from medieval times. He wears a loose white shirt, has blonde hair, and has light blue eyes.

Eric smiles at us and waves at Peter. Lucas looks at both of us from top to toe with a hint of disgust. Henry looks at me with his icy eyes.

I regret asking Peter to check if they have changed.

"Peter! How are you doing?" Eric asks Peter. "I should apologize for my behavior back then... Sorry I was so mean to everyone."

Peter smiles at him and holds out his hand. "That's alright," he tells him. "Peace?"

Eric stands up, his smile widening. "Peace!" he says, shaking Peter's hand.

I don't think Eric and Peter would start dating, so I'll let it slide.

Eric gestures to the table. "Come sit with us! Both of you! We don't mind."

Peter and I gladly take the offer and sit down. I sit next to Henry while Peter sits next to Eric.

We sit in awkward silence for a while. Eric starts a small conversation with Peter. They talk while the rest of us stay quiet.

I'm starting to doubt my thoughts about him.

"Aren't you that clumsy idiot that keeps coming every day?" Henry suddenly asks me.

We turn to him and then to me. I press my lips together and nod. "Yes, nice to meet you."

It's not really nice to meet you, dipshit.

"Ah, so you're the person who once cried his eyes out!" Lucas says.

I glance at Peter. He seems surprised with a hint of concern. I swallow once and nod again.

I gulp down my coffee and get up. "Yeah, that's me. I'm John, by the way. I need to call someone." I turn to Peter and pat his shoulder before walking into the pouring rain.

I don't mind the water wetting my clothes. I need the refreshment.

"You're so weird. Did you know that?"

I looked around but saw no one who was talking to me. "What?"

I sigh and lean against the wall. "Great, I'm hearing voices again," I mumble.

"Yep! Pretty stupid, right?"

"Leave me alone."

"Why? Afraid that I'd kill you?"

I groan and want to go back inside but stop. I see Peter arguing with Henry and Lucas. Eric seems to try to stop them.

Peter hits the table and turns to the door, looking at me. His eyes widen slightly before lowering his gaze. He walks toward me.

Before leaving the building, Peter grabs our umbrella.

He looks at me and says: "I got mad at them. Don't worry about it."

Peter smiles at me. I take a step forward and hug him tightly.

I feel his arm embracing me while his other arm keeps us dry as it holds the umbrella.

He places his head on my shoulder and nuzzles it slightly.

"I needed this..." he mumbles into my jacket. It makes me chuckle slightly.

"What did they do?" I ask him. "Perhaps keep it down. The stalker could be around."

Peter pulls away and looks at me with a small smile. "Oh-ho-ho! Cheesecake, you're adorable when you're worried."

"Am not, Pudding!" I hiss back.

We both laugh slightly.

"Okay, I got mad at them because of what they had said to you," Peter explains, whispering. "Eric did try to help, but that failed. It does seem like he has changed."

I grab his hand and squeeze it gently. "Anything else?"

Peter shakes his. "No, nothing," he tells me. He smiles. "Thank you for caring."

"Of course! You're always there for me!"   .

"Speaking of... How do you feel?"

I fall quiet for a moment. Thoughts fill my mind on how to answer that. I don't know why, but I'm crying.

Tears slide down my cheeks. I wipe them away as quickly as possible, but more follow.

I clear my throat, trying to get myself together. I look away, ashamed of myself.

Peter takes my hand, stopping me from wiping away my tears. "Let it out, Cheesecake. It's okay."

Without thinking, I go back and hug him harder than before. I don't know why, but I start sobbing. I can't seem to stop. Was I holding all of this?

I bury my face into his shoulder. Peter shuts the umbrella and drops it. He wraps his arms around me and hugs me back tightly.

"It just feels like everything I do is so wrong..." I mumble into his jacket through soft sobs. "All the things I do are bad...so bad..."

Peter hushes me softly, running a gentle hand through my hair. "Everything is alright. Just let it out."

We stand there, hugging. It feels like hours pass by.

"I'm so sorry for everything..." I whisper.

"Now, hush, little baby, don't you cry," Peter softly sings.

He manages to make me chuckle softly between sobs.

"Everything gonna be alright," he continues.

"Shut it, Peter!" I say.

He chuckles and messes up my hair. "Aw. Little Cheesecake is mad."

I hit his bicep. "Meany!"

Peter and I pull away from each other. I wipe away my last tears and smile at him.

"I would do anything for you, Peter," I tell him softly. "You mean so much to me."

He smiles and gives me another hug. "And I would do anything for you too, buddy."

"Can I go around free, or am I supposed to be watched the whole time?" I ask Peter.

Peter shrugs. "Not sure." He looks around. "Marcus isn't around, and you'd be fine. Well, hopefully."

I scoff. "Hopefully? Really? Relax, I will be fine."

Peter sighs. "Alright. Whatever you say. I trust you completely. But still. Be careful."

"Yeah, yeah! I know and will be careful."

Peter nods once with a smile. "Be at Jackson's place at 2 p.m., alright?"

"Alright. See you there!"

I turn around and walk away, leaving Peter in front of the café. I turn the corner and search for a clothing shop.

Chapter 18

Walking down the street, I look at the windows by the shops.

I stop by a store where they sell skater and motorcycle gear and clothes.

The window display had mannequins with leather jackets, black jeans, and gloves. I needed a new pair of gloves, so I went inside.

There were some people inside. There was air conditioning, making it a bit colder.

My gaze directly falls upon a pair of black gloves. Sadly, they were fingerless. I shrug and take them anyway.

A worker comes up to me. "Hello, can I help you with anything, sir?" he asks me.

I smile at him and reply: "Oh, yes, please. I'm looking for black gloves." I show him the fingerless ones. "With fingers."

The worker nods and gestures to a rack of gloves. "There are several gloves made from different materials. Feel free to look around."

I nod once to thank him and look at the rack. I look at a pair of leather gloves. "I'll take these," I tell the worker, turning to him.

He nods and walks to the counter. I follow.

"That would be twenty dollars," he tells me.

I take out my money and hand him the cash.

"Need a bag?"

I shake my head in response. I take the gloves and wear them. Saying goodbye to the worker, I leave the store.

I walk back to the café, hoping Peter has already gone somewhere else.

In front of the café, I see Eric, Henry, and Lucas. I see Henry and Lucas shouting or arguing with Eric. He doesn't seem happy and has tears in his eyes.

The thought of him loving Peter fades away. "Hm... Just a friend..." I mumble, walking toward them.

I step into an alleyway close enough to hear them.

"Why are you getting so soft on people?" I hear Henry shout at Eric.

"W-well, maybe because I'm sick of bullying!" Eric shouts back, trying to be confident.

I look around, trying to find any object to hit them with. Surprisingly, there's a baseball bat between cardboard boxes.

Without hesitation, I grab it and swing it around a bit. It's wood. The gloves give me a tight grip on the bat.

I focus on the shouting again.

"Shut the fuck up, Eric!" Lucas yells. "It's over! We're going."

"W-what?" Eric asks. "A-after all these years...you just go like that?"

I hear Eric getting pushed against a window.

I hear footsteps walking toward me. I hide behind the dumpster with my hood on, holding onto the bat tightly.

The rain pours and pours. It doesn't seem to stop. Not many people are walking on the streets.

Perfect for a kill.

As soon as I hear them pass the alley, I stay down and wait. Eric doesn't seem to be following.

I get up and leave the alley. The rain is a cover for my footsteps.

"Goodness," Henry yawns. "I wanted to get rid of him."

Lucas scoffs and runs a hand through his messy hair. "No shit! He was getting soft."

We stopped at a red light. I looked around to see if anyone was around. To my surprise, the streets were empty. It's probably because of the dog weather.

I clear my throat, trying to get their attention, which I get. I grin.

"Am I bothering, gentlemen?" I ask, moving the bat in circular motions while keeping it pointing down. I glance over at them. "We've met before. Remember me?"

The two look at each other and back at me. "You're that freak, John, aren't you?" Henry asks me.

I clench my jaw and tighten my grip around the bat. "Oh, you know how to make a man angry, don't you?" I say. "Well, I'm sure this is a big surprise for you."

Finally, I turn my body to them.

Lucas rolls his eyes. "You don't scare us, asshole. Leave."

I chuckle slightly, looking down at the bat. "What if I don't?"

"Then we'll just beat the crap out of you, freak," Henry threatens. "leave."

My chuckle turns into laughter. It's not an ordinary laugh. It's the laugh of a madman. I surprised myself with it.

Lucas starts feeling uncomfortable and takes a step back, nearly bumping into Henry.

I point the bat at Lucas. "Well, who's first?" I ask, pointing it at Henry now.

I lick my lips wet and wait for their answer. "I'm going to enjoy this so much."

Henry gives Lucas a push. He swallows and holds up his fists.

"Honestly," I say, looking down at his hands. "I expected more from you."

I lower the bat and step away. I place the bat near the building and turn back to them. "Show me what you got, dickhead."

I spread my arms, asking for the punch.

Lucas takes a step forward and punches me right in the face. The hit stings a little, and I'm sure it'll be a black eye.

I wet my lips with my tongue, wiping away the rain from my forehead. I take off my hood, revealing my head.

"Wait... Are you the-"

"Murderer from the news?" I finished Henry's sentence. I chuckle slightly, licking a drop of blood from my nose. "Yes. Yes, I am."

Lucas drops his arms to his side as his eyes widen. He grabs Henry by his arm, shaking it slightly. I laugh as I see his reaction.

Some people may look tough. But when you break through their cover, you see how weak they really are.

I nod at Henry. He swallows hard as he lowers his gaze. "Show me what you got!" I shout at him. "Or are you too afraid? Are you going to cry?"

I put my hood back on, making sure no one saw my face except Lucas and Henry. I turn to grab the bat.

Someone hits me on the back of my head. I'll be getting lots of bruises from today. I groan, annoyed, and look back.

Henry puts his hands up, ready to punch me another time.

I grip the bat tightly and lift it, letting him know that I will use it. He takes a step back, his hands trembling slightly.

"Do you fear death?" I ask curiously. "Do you think everything would go black? That you would drown in an endless sea of darkness? Or do you believe in Heaven and Hell? Going down into the burning flames or going up to the brightest light?"

I look at Lucas, grinning slightly. "What about you?" I ask him.

Lucas reaches for his back pocket. I punish him by hitting his elbow with the bat.

He steps back and pulls back his hand, holding up a gun. I'm slightly startled at the sight of the unexpected weapon.

I hold up my hands and drop the bat. "Alright, alright." I nod at the gun. "A Glock 17?"

"Ready to shoot a fucking hole through your damn head!" Lucas shouts. He looks at Henry. "Call the cops."

Henry gets out his phone and starts dialing 911. I hear the phone ring as I take a step forward.

"Stop!" Lucas shouts, his hands trembling. "Stop right there, or I'll shoot!"

I stop and look him in the eyes. "Shoot me."

"911. What's your emergency?" the phone goes.

I feel a slight feeling of concern.

What would happen if they knew it was me?

"Busted, freak!" the voice in my head shouts. "Kill him! Kill him! Kill him!"

"Shut up," I mumble.

I hear a click within the gun.

I step forward again as Henry starts talking to the officer on the phone. Lucas's hands tremble a bit more than before with each step I take.

"Stand back!" he shouts at me. I grin. "I will shoot!"

I'm close enough but don't say a word. I glance at the gun and back at Lucas. Finally, I say: "Don't talk too much and just kill the prey."

I grab him by the wrist, pulling him toward me. I grab his gun as he trips over my foot. He falls to the ground, and I shoot him in the head.

Thunder strikes as the clouds darken once again.

I turn to Henry. He stands still like a statue in fear. He looks at the dead body of his pal. His chest rises and lowers with each ragged breath.

In the distance, I see a car coming toward us. I clear my throat and get Henry's attention. "Poor, poor, Henry. You shouldn't be so mean to me and my love. Hang up."

He shakes his head and says the street where we're at. I clench my jaw. I grab him by his shirt collar and throw him on the street.

The sound of screeching brakes fills the surroundings.

Henry got thrown forcefully across the street. The car stops, and the lights turn off.

The driver gets out of the car and runs toward Henry's body. I slowly step toward them.

The driver looks at me. "Call 911!" he tells me. "Maybe we can still save him!"

I shake my head. "I don't want that," I reply. "And I don't want any witnesses too."

I hold up my gun at the man's forehead and pull the trigger. His body falls to the ground next to Henry.

I take a good look at Henry. That car must've hit him hard. His tibia bone has torn through his skin. His eyes are wide open, staring into emptiness. I watch as his blood mixes with the rain and the blood of the driver.

Dropping the gun by the driver's hand, I step back, turn, and step into an alley.

CHAPTER 19

I take off my gloves and hood. I check my phone and see that it's an hour to 2 p.m.

Placing my phone back into my pocket, I realize that there are drops of blood on my clothes.

Sighing, I hope they won't notice it. I do need to come up with something to hide any suspicion. Looking around, I think of what I could do.

Peter is still sick, so I think of something that might cheer him up.

I enter a clothing store and look around.

I'm not sure what his clothing size is. My gaze falls upon a hoodie. I walk toward it and feel the dark blue fabric. It feels soft and stretchy.

It has a zipper dividing the pocket in two.

I took a large one, thinking it would fit Peter.

I continued to walk around the store, thinking of what I could do.

On a small table, I see multiple neckties and bow ties.

Would he wear it if I bought it for him?

I have a look at a couple of ties, trying to find the perfect one for him. He looks good in everything.

His slightly muscular body under that white shirt of his... I want to kiss it and caress it as if it's the last thing I do. The thought of it makes me blush slightly.

I need to get the thoughts out of my mind, but I can't help but think of the other night. He may not have liked it, but I loved the sight.

Clearing my throat, I try to focus on what I'm doing.

A silk black tie with thin gray lines catches my eye. I hold it up and feel the fabric. It's soft and smooth.

Next to the table, there are multiple tie clips. I pick out a gold-colored one and take a good look at it.

I'm sure he'll like it.

I step away from the table and go to the cashier.

"Good day, sir. Got everything you wanted?" the woman behind the counter asks me with a smile.

I smile back and nod. "Yes, I did," I reply, placing everything on the counter.

The woman takes them and scans them, calculating how much they'll cost.

"That would be sixty-seven dollars, please."

I nod once again and hand her the money. She takes it and takes out a bag. She gives me the bag and says: "Have a nice day further, sir."

"You too, miss," I reply. I turn to the door and leave the building.

No one noticed the blood. I'm sure Peter, Marcus, and Anastasia won't notice it.

I wanted to apologize to my sister, so I entered the flower shop. The florist from last time greets me with a smile.

I wave awkwardly and look around. I take a bouquet of white roses and bring it to the counter.

"New flowers?" he asks me.

"These are for my sister," I reply, smiling slightly. "I need to apologize to her."

The florist nods and takes the bouquet. "Ribbon?"

"Red one, please."

I watch as he takes out a red ribbon and ties the flowers.

"That would be six dollars, please."

I take out the money and hand it to him. "Thank you, and have a nice day further, sir," I say.

I turn to the door and leave the store. Small drops of rain fall from the sky as I walk back to Jackson's place.

In the distance, I can hear multiple police cars' sirens.

I get back to Jackson's place and open the door. A shiver runs down my spine as I feel the sudden temperature change.

José and Juliette are standing in the kitchen with Anastasia. Jackson, Alexander, and Jasmin are probably in Jackson's room. And Marcus and Peter are sitting on the couch.

I chuckle slightly at the sight of Peter being wrapped into a blanket like a burrito.

"Not a word," Peter says, slightly grumpy. He coughs. "Rain sucks."

My chuckles turn into laughter. I shut the door, shaking my head. I take off my shoes and jacket.

"How do you feel?" Marcus asks me. "Did anything happen?"

I shake my head, turning to them. "Everything's fine, Marcus," I reply.

He nods, satisfied by my answer. I step toward them and place the bag of clothes in front of Peter, smiling slightly. "That should keep you warm."

As Peter looks confused at the bag, I turn to the kitchen and walk toward my sister. I hold out the bouquet with my gaze slightly lowered. "Sorry..." I mumble. "I hope you can forgive me."

Juliette takes the bouquet in silence. I look at her once before dropping my gaze once again. I step back and walk to Peter.

He looks up at me as I sit down next to him. "What's in the bag?" he asks.

I take the bag and place it on Peter's lap. Peter takes a look at it before opening it. His grumpy, questioning expression changes into a happy one. He holds up the hoodie. "You bought me a hoodie!"

Chuckling softly, I pat his shoulder. "I didn't know what your size was, so I hope a large is alright," I tell him. "Do you like it?"

He looks at me, his smile widening brightly. "Do I like it? What do you think? I love it!" he tells me.

I smile, knowing that he's happy.

It only makes me regret things more and more.

Peter stands up, dropping the blanket onto the floor. He opens the hoodie and puts it on. Turning around, he closes the zipper.

His smile is so childish. I love it.

He spreads his arms and asks: "And?"

"Looks alright," Marcus says. "Large."

Peter drops his arms, laughing softly. "Well, duh!"

Peter takes the bag, looking inside it again with surprise. "There's more?" He opens it, his eyes widening slightly. "A tie and clip?"

He takes them out of the bag and holds the tie in the light. "It looks amazing," he says. "I will wear this. Both."

He gestures to me to stand up, and I do it. Peter spreads his arms and takes me in. He seems happy with his gifts.

We let go of each other, smiling brightly.

Someone clears her throat. I turn to see who it is, and see Juliette with her arms crossed looking at me.

I take a deep breath before gesturing to the door. "How about we talk about this outside?" I ask.

She nods and places the bouquet on the counter. Without a word, she walks right past me.

I followed and shut the door, leaving everyone speechless inside.

My sister sits on the now-wet sidewalk, waiting for me. I hesitate slightly.

"Are you coming, John?" Juliette asks me, patting the spot next to her.

I know she can't see me, but I nod in response before stepping toward her.

We sit in silence, watching as kids bike past us. Tiny drops of water fall from the sky as a slight fog falls upon the town.

I look down at my lap, thinking of what Juliette might say. I finally find the courage to look at her.

She looks at me with pleading eyes. "Tell me you lied."

My lips thinned as I thought of an answer. I sigh deeply, brushing a hand over my face, and pause at my mouth. I look at the street. "I don't know what to say..."

"Start with apologizing, stupid." She hits my arm. "Apologize!"

I look at her. Her hits didn't really hurt, but it felt like a herd of gazelles stormed right at me. Her eyes are filled with tears as she looks into mine. "Tell me you lied..."

As gently as possible, I cup her face. She pulled away slightly, making me flinch. But then she leaned into my touch as tears rolled down her cheeks.

I wipe them away with my thumbs, letting her take all the time she needs. "I'm sorry, my sweet sister," I whisper. I kiss her forehead. "My love is different than others... My jealousy is different from others..."

Juliette looks right at me with her teary eyes. "Y-you're sick... Sick in t-the head," she tells me between sobs. "We need to tell Marcus. You need to tell him."

Sighing again, I shake my head. "I can't." I kiss her forehead again. "As much as I try to, the voice in my head tells me no."

She pulls away, looking away from me. I see the disappointment in her eyes. "Then you should tell José," she tells me. "He's the oldest."

I run a hand through my hair. "I know, I know. I'm not sure how he would react." I chuckle slightly. "He'd be so disappointed that the youngest member of the family, is a murderer."

Juliette hits my cheek. I freeze for a moment, trying to process what just happened. She just slapped me. "You're an idiot," she tells me. "A bloody idiot."

I press my lips together and nod. "That's mean."

"Not as mean as not telling your brother a big crime."

"I'm not ready!"

"Then not as bad as murdering three people!"

My teeth grit, and I ball fists. "Add three more!"

Juliette falls quiet. I can feel her gaze upon me. I glared at her, and she was indeed staring wide-eyed at me.

I sigh deeply and soften my gaze. "If I'm right, Marcus, Peter, or Anastasia would say something soon. Glock 17, GSW, car accident, et cetera."

My sister's eyes widened even more as her jaw dropped. She gulped hard, and I saw her hands clenching her pants. "T-tell me you didn't..."

"I did, Juliette. I did."

I feel bad when she looks at me with those eyes. She looks at me with pure disgust.

"Sister..."

"Shut it. Save it. I don't care. Just tell José." She gets up and walks back to the door. I look right in front of me at the streets. "John." I turn my head to Juliette. She's looking at me. "Tell me if you do something else."

I force a small smile and nod. "I will, sister. No worries."

Juliette nods once before turning to the door and entering. I'm left alone with my thoughts outside.

Just when I thought it couldn't get worse, the rain started pouring again.

I sigh deeply and stay in the rain, not wanting to go inside.

"See? She hates you!" the voice in my head tells me. "She hates you! She hates you! Ha ha ha! She hates you! She hates you!"

Groaning, I wipe away the rain from my eyes. "Shut up. I don't want your company."

"Peter will only love you if you kill for him... He'd love hearts and flowers!"

This time, I stay quiet and think about it. I've never thought of something like that.

Would he really love a heart?

I take out the knife from my boot and look at it.

I can try to give him a heart.

CHAPTER 20

There's a knock heard from behind me. I turn to look who it is. Peter stands by the door with an umbrella. Behind him are Marcus and Anastasia. "John, I think it'll be better if you'd come inside," Peter says. "It's cold outside."

Peter walks toward me. He's still wearing the blue sweater I bought him, making me smile slightly.

The umbrella covers us both. "Please, come inside."

I smile at him and stand up, running a hand through my wet hair. "For how long was I out here?" I ask, forgetting the time.

"You were out here for thirty minutes after Juliette went inside," Marcus says, walking toward us. He has no umbrella, so the rain wets his shirt slightly. "Come inside, John. You'll get cold." His tone is concerning.

"Oh..." I look down and nod. "I didn't know, sorry."

Peter slightly bumps my arm, making me look at him. "It's alright, Cheesecake."

I smile at him and turn to Marcus. "Shall we go inside?" I ask.

Marcus and Peter both nod once. Marcus steps aside and gestures to the door, letting us go first. The three of us walk back inside.

The smell of tea filled my nose the moment we entered. In the kitchen, Anastasia and José are brewing tea.

"Green?" I ask, trying to guess the tea by the smell.

Anastasia chuckles slightly and answers with a smile: "You really are an expert."

José doesn't really smile. He glances once at me and then back at the boiling water. I look around for my sister and find her leaning against the hallway wall. She cocks her head, and I directly know what she means.

I narrow my eyes as I clench my jaw and form fists. I feel a rage of anger washing over me.

"John?" someone asks softly.

"What?" I ask furiously. I flinched slightly and softened my gaze. "Peter..."

I see him gulp and lower his gaze as he takes a small step back. I feel bad when I see his reaction, so I gently take his hand. "Sorry that I yelled at you."

He nods and replies: "It's alright. Just tell me. What's wrong?"

"I..." I started thinking of what I could say. I glance at my siblings before looking back at Peter. "I did something bad."

Peter tilts his head in confusion. "What do you mean?" he asks me. "How bad is it?"

"It's bad."

Marcus places his hand on my shoulder. I turn my head to him. "What did you do?"

Taking a deep breath, I force a slight smile. "It's nothing to worry about!"

I turn to the kitchen and walk to the stove. I open the cabinet when I realize that the thermometer isn't in the water. I gently place it in the water, measuring the heat.

They've already placed the tea leaves in the water, which caused the aroma to fill the rooms.

I take a big coaster from one of the drawers and place it on the counter.

Carefully, I place the pot on the coaster.

"Tell me about it." I look to my right, where José is leaning against the counter. "Tell me," José repeats.

Sighing, I shake my head. "Not here." I turn back to the water.

José turns me back to him, grabbing me by my shoulders. "Tell. Me."

"No," I answer dryly. I turn back to the tea and stir it slightly.

"What are you two talking about?" Anastasia asks us. I forgot she was here.

I shrug and slightly smile as I look at her. "It's nothing to worry about, Anastasia. It's family business."

She nods, understanding.

José grabs me by my shoulders again and turns me to him. "Nadie habla español excepto nosotros. Dímelo. (No one speaks Spanish except us. Tell me.)"

"Sabía que te enfadarías conmigo. Por eso no quería decírtelo. (I knew you'd be mad at me. That's why I didn't want to tell you.)"

"You're a monster."

I slam my hand on the table. "I'm not a monster! I'm not! I'm not! I'm not!"

There's a sudden shock on José's face. Then I realized why. I feel a sudden heat hit my skin. I look at my hand.

It's in the boiling tea.

"Damn it..." I mumble.

I take my hand out of the water and watch as my skin turns red. Peter takes my wrist and opens the faucet quickly. The cool water hits my skin.

The slight pain fades after a while.

Anastasia takes the medical kit out of the bathroom cabinet. They put some ointment on the burn. It feels cold. They put a damp cloak on it and bandaged it.

They helped me get to the couch even though I said that I didn't need assistance.

They got me a mug of tea, but it had gotten cold already. I can't help but think of why it didn't hurt. It was boiling, and yet it didn't hurt.

"How do you feel?" Jackson asks me as he sits down next to me.

I shrug. "I'm fine," I say with a small smile. Jasmine and Alexander sit on the ground in front of the TV. And the rest sit on the couches around me, with Peter next to me.

I take a sip from the tea and lick my lips.

A phone rings. Everyone turns to Marcus. He looks at the phone and gets up. "Sorry, I need to take this one."

He walks toward the kitchen and answers the phone. His last words I understood were: "Slow down. Tell me what the emergency is."

I'm sure it's about the murders from before.

I look at Juliette and José. They're looking right at me with a suspicious glare.

"Dime que no se trata ti. (Tell me it's not about you.)" José says.

I sigh and run a hand through my hair. "No lo sé. (I don't know.)" I reply. "Puede que si. Puede que no. (Maybe. Maybe not.)"

"What are you two talking about?" Jasmine asks us.

"No one understands this shit!" Jackson shouts. "Tell us!"

I groan and sink into the couch. "Why do people keep telling me to tell them things?"

I feel a hand on my head. I look up and see Peter smiling at me. "You're adorable, Cheesecake."

I swallow slightly, feeling my cheeks flush. "Oh, shut it, Pudding."

I sit up and lean against him, placing my head on his shoulder. He runs his hand through my hair, petting me gently.

Marcus comes back to us. We all look at him. He looks at Peter and me and asks: "You two sure you aren't dating?"

Jackson grins evilly and says: "Oh, let them be, Marcus. They're obsessed with each other!"

"You would be surprised!" Juliette says.

Everyone turns to my siblings.

"What do you mean?" Peter asks. He looks back at me, placing his hand on my shoulder. "What are they talking about?"

I blink a couple of times since I don't know how to answer. I look at my siblings. "I don't know what you mean."

"You know what we mean, John!" José shouts at me.

I stand up, gently brushing Peter's hand off my shoulder. I look at Marcus and ask: "What was the call about? Was it the stalker?"

He nods. "Yes, it was. How did you guess?"

I shrug. "A guess since you're a detective of our case. What was it about?"

"Another three murders."

"How did you know it was the stalker?"

He looks at Peter. "Do you know someone named Eric?"

I can hear Peter gulp as he hears his name. "Henry and Lucas?"

"Dead."

Peter takes a deep breath and slides a hand over his face. "Who's the third?"

"A driver got killed with a Glock 17. Henry got killed with the same gun, but Lucas got hit by the car." Marcus looks back at me. "He left the weapons. I say it in plural because there was a bat and the Glock 17."

I shake my head, sighing deeply. "How's Eric?"

"Shocked, but he'll be alright," Marcus says. "He followed a police car because he knew the direction Henry and Lucas were going."

I turn to Peter and squeeze his shoulder slightly. "It'll be alright, Pudding. We'll catch him soon."

Peter looks up at me with a small smile tugging on the corner of his lips. "I thought I was the cop who needed to comfort you."

I look at my mug. "How about I'll make elderberry tea for you?" I ask, looking back at Peter. I place the back of my hand on his forehead. "You still have that cold."

His smile widens as he says: "Go ahead, Mr. Tea expert."

We both quietly laugh.

I take my mug and go to the kitchen.

Pouring the tea down the drain, I think to myself: "I'm willing to kill anyone for you, Peter Quintin."

CHAPTER 21

I walk down the streets through the rain. I can't be the only one thinking that Autumn is coming.

I enter the café and look around for Peter. He told me he had something important to say.

It's been a few days since the last murders. It got in the newspaper. I'm not sure if I should be happy or not that I got into the papers.

"Cheesecake!" I hear someone say. I turn to the door and see Peter standing there in a thin jacket, and I can see the blue hood of the hoodie. "Sorry if I kept you waiting."

Shaking my head slightly, I smile and say: "It's alright. I'm always the one waiting."

Peter steps closer and hugs me tightly. I hug him back because I don't know what else I can do, and I love doing it.

We let go and looked at each other in silence. I chuckle slightly and scratch the back of my neck as it starts to get awkward. Peter quietly laughs at my reaction.

"You're adorable, Cheesecake," he tells me with a widening smile.

I bite my lower lip slightly and tug my pants slightly, feeling embarrassed. "Oh, hush, Pudding."

Peter laughs again and pats my shoulder. "Latte?"

"Black with two packages of sugar plus a package of milk?"

He raises both eyebrows, frowning slightly. "You memorized my orders?"

I smirk and reply: "What can I say? I have a good memory."

Peter rolls his eyes and scoffs. "Yeah, yeah, smartass." He chuckles with the last word.

I nod at the counter.

We both walk together to the counter. As Peter orders our coffee, somehow, I feel multiple eyes watching our every move.

"Is that everything?" the cashier asks.

"A croissant, maybe," Peter says. I look confused at him, and he looks at me.

"Did you just say quackson?" I ask him, frowning with a smile.

Peter groans, hitting my bicep. "Oh, shut it. I always pronouns croissant that way."

I nod, squinting my eyes slightly.

"Shut. Up!" Peter shouts, hitting my bicep again. His warm smile stays on his face. It lights up my world. He turns to the cashier. "Make that two croissants."

The cashier nods with a smile, clearly enjoying the show. He gets out two plates and two cups.

I look to my right, where I see Peter humming quietly to the café's music with his eyes nearly shut. A small smile lingers on his lips as he does.

I can't help but stare at the handsome man before me. He's so muscular, calm, and confident. Multiple things that I can't be.

Yes, I can kill a man with my bare hands, but I could never have the same feelings as him.

Our coffee is ready. Peter takes out his card, but I place my hand on his and lower it. He looks at me with a questioning look. I smile in response. "I'll pay today."

"Is everything alright?" Peter asks me. "You never do this."

I shrug and nod. "I'm just in the mood, Pudding." I take out my card and pay for our food and drinks.

In the corner of my eye, I can see Peter looking at my every move. I take our cups. "Will you take the plates?" I ask, turning to him.

He snaps awake and takes the plates quickly, making me laugh slightly. "And you call me adorable," I tease him.

"Because you are!" Peter reacts. "But you're also a pain!" he adds, half laughing.

I scoff and roll my eyes. "Come on." We both walk toward a free table by the window and sit down.

Peter takes a knife from the tray of cutlery. I pass him the butter as I see him do it. "Am I that predictable?" he asks.

I shrug. "I have two things in my head called eyes."

We both laugh at my answer.

Peter butters his croissant while I eat mine without the butter. I look outside at the pouring rain. It reminds me of bullets. Small bullets.

"Do you think that stalker is watching us right now?" Peter suddenly asks me.

My breath slightly hitches as he mentions it. I look at him, thinking of an answer. I start looking around, acting like I'm looking for someone.

"I don't think he's watching," Peter says. "And even if he was here, this is a café. He wouldn't be able to do much."

I focus on him again. "I guess you're right," I softly say.

Under the table, I feel Peter's leg brush against mine. From the way he looks at me, I see that he's trying to comfort me.

"How have you been feeling lately?" he asks me. "The office is quite busy, I'm not going to lie."

I smile slightly and nod. "Yeah, very busy." I look down at my croissant and sigh.

More cops come in and out of that office. The more murders, the more officers come. It gets busier every day.

I didn't mean to, but I killed one again.

What am I saying? I did mean it. And I enjoyed every second. Every scream. Every beg. I loved it.

I got mad because she loved Peter. I had to punish her for trying to take him away from me.

Juliette wasn't happy with it, and so was José. I can still hear his shouts in the back of my mind every time I think about it. And he slapped me. My brother hit me multiple times.

I blink a couple of times and look at Peter, his eyes filled with concern. "Are you sure you're alright, John?" he asks me.

He said my name. He doesn't say it a lot lately, only when he's serious.

Clearing my throat, I nod and say: "Yes, I'm alright. Just thinking."

Peter takes my hand and squeezes it gently. I take a deep breath and rub the back of his hand with my thumb.

All I want is to kiss him. It's killing me inside, knowing that I can't do it.

A man walks over to us. He squeezed Peter's shoulder, causing him to look at the man. "Can I help you, sir?" Peter asks the man.

"I just wanted you to know that you look handsome," the man answers. He chuckles shyly. "Your eyes are more beautiful from up close."

Peter smiles. "Well, thank you, sir. That's quite nice of you to say."

The man nods, his smile widening.

I guess that's my next target.

The man walks toward the counter, probably to order some coffee.

I watch his every movement. I look if he compliments any other people. But he doesn't.

"John?" Peter says, dragging me back to reality.

I clear my throat and look at him. "Sorry, I must've dozed off." I smile slightly before looking at my cup of coffee. "Don't you think it's weird that a random man comes up to compliment you?"

Peter looks back at the man and back at me. He has his thinking face on. "Now that you say it, I think you're right."

I let go of Peter's hand and sat up. I finish my croissant quickly and take a sip of my coffee.

Peter finishes his croissant and glares back at the man. There's a notification sound heard. Peter looks at his jacket before taking out his phone.

He frowns slightly.

"What's wrong?" I ask him.

Peter puts away his phone, turns back to me with a smile, and replies: "It's nothing to worry about."

I tilt my head slightly in suspicion. "Who just texted you?" I ask.

"It's Marcus," Peter says. "He just checked if everything was okay."

I shake my head. "He never does that." I lean forward and cross my arms on the table. "Who was it, Peter?"

"I want to leave the café," he replies. "I don't think it's safe right now." I see his eyes trail back off to the man in the corner.

I nod in response and get up. Taking my jacket, I see Peter distracted as he does the same. I grab one of the knives from the table and hide it.

We both leave the café. We take a different route because there may be the 'stalker'.

When we get to a red light, I look at the street we just came from. Between the crowd, I see the man from the café following.

I get near Peter's ear and whisper: "That man is following us."

Peter gulps as I see his eyes searching for the man.

The light turns green. I tap Peter's bicep to get his attention.

We continue walking.

As we walk by an alleyway, I grab Peter's shoulders and pull him with me into the alley.

We look at each other, my hands still gripping his shoulders. "I want you to stay here," I tell him. "I will just talk to him. Nothing bad can happen."

"But-"

"Stay here. I promise everything will be okay."

I look at him for a bit, making sure he's alright. Finally, he nods as he approves.

I smile at him before leaving without another word.

I leave the alleyway and end up on the streets from where we came from. I look around for the man and see him entering a different alley on the other side of the street.

Without thinking, I cross the streets to follow.

At the beginning of the alley, I realize how dark it is. I squinted my eyes, trying to look clearer. I see him in the middle of the alley with his back facing me.

Slowly, I approached him, grasping the knife from beneath my jacket.

"Who are you?" the mysterious man asks me without turning around.

I continue walking, holding the knife pointing down at the ground, ignoring his question.

Suddenly, the man reaches for his hair and takes it off. It seems that he was wearing a wig all along.

Surprised by his sudden actions, I stopped for a moment, trying to identify him.

I hear him sigh audibly. He runs a hand through his hair. "Answer me."

"John Welling is my name," I say sternly, keeping my eyes on him.

His hand stops. "John?" he asks with a surprised tone. He stays quiet for a while. "So what they said is true?"

I tighten my grip on the knife. "Who are you?" I ask.

He turns, revealing his face. I freeze when. I see the man standing before me. I shake my head in disbelief.

"Step into the light!" I shout.

The man does as I told him, and he steps into the light.

A sudden fear hits me. I want to run. "Marcus..." I mumble. My breath quickens.

"I wish it wasn't you, John," he says, looking at me with disappointment. "But you know what happens next."

"Uh-oh! Busted!" the voice in my head says.

"Shut it, Turkey!" I shout. I've called the voice Turkey since he wouldn't stop blabbing like one.

"There's no one else here, John," Marcus tells me, causing me to look at him.

I nod and point the knife at him. "I know that, detective. It's just Turkey that keeps blabbing and talking in my head."

Marcus looks at the knife I'm holding. I'm standing with it in front of a detective, a friend. I wanted to kill him. I wanted to skin him while he was still conscious.

I gulp down my feelings and turn, wanting to run, but I freeze. My breath hitches as I see them.

Multiple cops are pointing loaded guns at me, blocking the exit. Anastasia and Peter stand in front of the group. Anastasia is pointing a gun at me.

Peter, on the other hand, stands still, looking at me with disbelief. I see a tear running down his cheek as I drop the knife. "Peter..." I say, almost whispering. "I-I can explain!"

I see him shake his head. "I could never love someone like you." His voice cracks as more tears come. He drops his gaze, shaking his head with disappointment.

"All I wanted is for you to love me..." I mumble. I look down at the knife. I crouch and take it. "Love me... Love me. Love me. Love me... " My hands tremble as I look at the knife.

"You're sick," Anastasia says. "We'll help you, John."

I shake my head and get back on my feet. "If I can't have you..." I start running toward Peter and pin him against the wall. "Then no one can!"

I tried stabbing him in the stomach but he stopped my hand. "All I wanted is to be loved!" I hiss.

A gun goes off. I drop the knife and fall onto my knees, too filled with anger to scream. Someone shot me in the fucking thighs.

"Kill them." the voice says. "Kill them all. They took your love away. Kill them."

I look up at Peter. His chest rises and falls with every breath. He doesn't run or ask for help. Does he want this?

I hear footsteps behind me. Someone grabs my wrists, and I feel him cuff one of them.

I pull my wrist away and grab the knife by my knees. I kicked the cop in his leg and cut his eye. He cries out in pain.

"Finish him!"

I hold up the knife, ready to strike.

Someone grabs my hands. I look up and see Peter. His eyes are wide and his breathing is ragged. He shakes his head desperately, not wanting to see me kill someone. "Please," he mouths.

I hear multiple men approach us, but they don't do anything yet. I exhale deeply and let go of the knife once again.

I've always hated to see Peter sad. His trembling hands let go of mine. I see multiple tears fall to the ground as he begins to sob. "How could you?" he asks between sobs. "I trusted you!"

"Poor Peter. You should've done better."

I look at the gun by the man.

"Is it loaded?" I ask.

The man covering his eye follows my gaze. "Why should I tell a monster like you?"

I smile and take the gun quickly. They tried to take it away but failed. I pulled the trigger and missed. My jaw clenches. I try again. And again someone pulled my arm away.

"Just let me die!" I shout as loud as possible. "Make me pay for all the murders I've done!"

Peter takes the gun and pushes me onto my stomach. He cuffs my hands. "I'm sorry..." I hear him whisper.

CHAPTER 22

After my trials and time in jail, they sent me to a mental hospital.

I didn't think it would work, but it does. I've been in here for four months already.

My brother and sister visit sometimes. Marcus came to check on me from time to time.

But there was no sign of Peter.

Marcus always told me he wanted to wait until he felt better.

My love for him never died.

The doctors took me to the meeting room and told me to wait, which I did. I sat there alone in the room.

The sound of the ticking clock was the only thing making a sound.

Finally, the door opens. I look up and see one of the doctors talking to someone. I listen with curiosity, trying to hear what they're saying.

The man steps aside and lets someone enter, someone in a suit with a tie and clip.

He smiles at me, his eyes glistening with hope.

I can't help but smile as I see him. He's wearing my gifts. I gesture to the chair before me. He sits.

The doctor stays in the room to check if we follow the rules.

The clock continues to count the seconds that pass. We stare at each other. Smile at each other.

Finally, I ask: "How are you doing, Peter?"

Peter exhales deeply, looking down at his lap, smiling widely. "I missed hearing your voice," he says, so soft that it's almost impossible to understand.

I want to take his hand and squeeze it, but I don't do it. I know that I'm not allowed to touch visitors.

"I've missed you too, Pudding," I tell him. "I've missed our coffee moments, your laugh, your smile, and your wonderful voice."

I see a tear run down Peter's cheek.

"I've always wanted to say that," I continue. "I've always wanted to tell you how much I love you."

Multiple tears ran down his cheeks as I told him I loved him. I hear him sniff slightly.

I can't resist.

As gently as possible, I take Peter's hands and kiss them softly.

The man in the corner steps toward us and says: "You aren't supposed to touch each other."

Peter nods and tries pulling his hand back, but I squeeze them gently. He looks at me as I shake my head.

I look at the doctor and say: "Please, we haven't seen each other in months."

"I'm sorry to hear that, but you know the rules, Mr. Welling," the doctor says.

I sigh and gently place Peter's hands on the table and stroke them with my thumb before letting go. "How would you feel when you didn't see your wife and kids for months and wasn't allowed to touch them?" I ask him.

He tilts his head. "How did you-"

"There's a ring around your middle finger, and your keys are hanging from your pocket with a keychain made by a kid," I tell him without taking my eyes off Peter's hands. "Anything else to say, or are you going to use that brain of yours?"

We hear him gulp. He shakes his head and steps back to the corner. Peter's lips thinned as he tried to contain his giggles.

"Come on, laugh," I say, smiling slightly. "I haven't heard that warm laugh of yours in months."

Peter suddenly gets up, causing the chair to fall over. He walks toward me. "Up," he says.

I look at him in confusion. I hear a soft chuckle escape the corner of his mouth. He takes my arm and pulls me to my feet.

He pulls me in his arms, eager to hug me. I can't help but sink into his embrace and hug him back.

I feel his wet cheek on my neck. I feel my eyes getting watery the longer we hug.

I missed his scent. His warmth. His everything. I could never forget what a hug with him feels like. I love the way his warmth hits my cold skin.

The door opens. I try pulling away, but Peter won't let me. I chuckle slightly and nuzzle into his neck. "You're adorable," I whisper.

He groans softly and replies: "Shut it, Cheesecake."

Even after saying that, he doesn't let go. Instead, he hugs me tighter.

I feel the tears rolling down my face.

Embarrassed, I hide my face in his shoulder.

After what feels like ages, we let go of each other.

I see a tear running down his face the moment we let go. Gently, I wipe it away with my thumb as I caress his face. He leans into my touch, widening my smile. I've always wanted him to do that.

We smile at each other as we stand there.

Finally, Peter looks at the person who just came in. He clears his throat and wipes away the remaining tears with the palms of his hands, stepping away from me.

I follow his gaze. I bite my bottom lip as I see who it is. I wipe away my tears with my sleeves and awkwardly say: "Good afternoon, Marcus."

He laughs quietly and replies: "Good afternoon, John." He looks at Peter. "Good seeing you again, Peter."

Peter clears his throat. "Hey, Marcus. I came early because I wanted to see him alone," Peter says.

Marcus nods understandingly. "Want some more time?"

I look at Peter, and he looks back at me. "No, it's okay," he says, nearly whispering. "Cheesecake and I can always talk later."

We smile at each other before sitting back down. Marcus takes a chair from the corner and places it next to Peter's before sitting down himself.

I glare at the doctor, who is still standing in the corner.

"How's everything going, John?' Marcus asks me, causing my attention to go back to them.

I smile and answer: "I'm doing alright. Thanks for asking." I cross my arms on the table. "How are things going?"

"Things are going great," Peter says. "Anastasia brings me tea every morning, thinking that it may cheer me up."

My smile widens. "What kind?" I ask, curious if he knows.

He licks his lips and scratches the back of his neck, sinking into the chair as he does. It makes me chuckle again.

"Is it better than mine?" I ask. "Do you miss mine?"

Peter groans and continues to sink into the chair. "I miss our coffee moment. I miss the way you look as you look at your tea... But no, your tea is way better."

This time, I laugh. "You're adorable!"

"No, I'm not!" he argues. "You are!"

"No, you are!"

"You!"

"You!"

"How about you both are adorable?" Marcus asks.

"Shut it, Marcus!" Peter and I shout in sync.

We both blink twice and look at each other. We start laughing out loud.

Marcus sits still with his lips tightly pressed together. "Okay," he mouths, clicking with a pen.

We calm down after a few seconds of laughter.

I clear my throat while Peter sits up straight again.

"Okay," Marcus says. "Now that that has passed, let's talk about businesses."

I sigh deeply, not wanting to talk about business.

"Hush, now, John. Time for business," Peter says with such an arrogant tone, smiling smugly.

I can't help but snort as I see him do it. I cover my mouth while I press my lips together.

Marcus sighs and covers his eyes with a small smile. "You two are the most adult yet childish people I know."

Peter and I burst out in laughter. I see Marcus's shoulders jerk as he chuckles along.

After all the laughter and jokes, we finally get to business.

I place a hand on my chin as I cross my arm, waiting for one of them to start. Marcus gets out a file, my file.

He opens it and goes to the things that lead to me.

"Okay, John," he starts. "How about we start talking about how everything started?" He smiles slightly. "Are you comfortable with that?"

I nod in response, waiting for them to ask questions I've been waiting to answer. I've been wanting to tell the truth for a long time.

Marcus places a recorder on the table. "In the alley, you told someone to shut up. Who did you say it to?" he asks.

Peter has taken a notebook and patiently clicks with the pen.

"Oh, that!" I say. I clear my throat. "I have a voice in my head which I called Turkey."

I watch as Peter scribbles things in his notebook. He stops and chews on the end of the pen. "Why did you call him Turkey?"

I smirk slightly. "Because he kept blabbing on and on like one."

"What did he or she say?" Marcus asks, leaning forward.

I think for a moment before answering. "In the alley, he told me to kill the cops. That's one of the reasons I snapped."

"One of the reasons?" Peter asks, not looking up from the notes as he writes. He frowns slightly, visibly being focused.

I smile as I see him do it. Marcus clears his throat, and I shake my head, trying to focus on the questions.

I look at him. "Where's your head at?" he asks me.

Peter looks up from his notes and looks at me.

"My head's on my shoulders," I tell them. "I just dozed off."

"Yeah, sure," Marcus says sarcastically. He sighs and shakes his head. "Eres un romántico empedernido. (You're a hopeless romantic.)"

Peter and I look surprised at him. Peter's jaw drops after a few seconds as he processes what just happened. Marcus chuckles at our reactions. "I may or not have googled some things."

"You need to work on your accent," I tell him. "¡No soy un romántico! (I'm not a romantic!)"

Marcus starts to laugh, and I chuckle slightly along. Peter watches us laugh in silence, still not understanding us.

After a bit, we stop laughing. Looking at Peter, I feel my cheeks flush slightly. I clear my throat and say: "Peter, you asked me a question earlier. Mind repeating that?"

He nods. "Yeah. You said that hearing the voice was one of the reasons why you snapped. What were the others?"

I lick my lips wet. "I was hopelessly in love with you." I shrug. "You said you could never fall in love with me. I felt an enormous amount of anger and disappointment rise inside me." I look down at my lap. "I wanted you. I needed you. And I was ready to murder anyone who would take you away."

I take a deep breath, shut my eyes, and try locking away any dark thoughts. I don't hear Peter scribble in his notebook.

I look up at them. They both look at me, visibly speechless. I swallow awkwardly and rub the back of my neck. "S-sorry. That was too much, wasn't it?"

Peter's lips thinned as his hand hovered over the notebook.

"What did you think of that night?" he asks.

Thinking, I tilt my head slightly. "What night?" I dig deep into my memory. "Oh, that night..."

I lick my lips as I think of the way he squirmed under my touch. I swallow hard. "In the bathroom, there's a ceiling panel loose." I thinned my lips. "I put the gloves I used there."

I hear Peter inhale sharply. I glance at him. He seems a bit uncomfortable and shifting in his chair.

"How about we talk about something else?" I request.

I've never liked seeing Peter uncomfortable or scared.

Peter nods and starts scribbling in his notebook again.

Marcus turns to another page in the file.

I patiently wait for them to ask me a question or finish this conversation.

"How did you manage to crush that man's head with a pipe or manage to break Hugo's arm?" Marcus asks. His expression betrays that he's genuinely surprised and curious.

I shrug. "I used to do martial arts when I was a kid," I tell them. "My father was an alcoholic. My mother wanted to protect me, so she sent me to the martial arts school."

I look at how they react. Peter's hand froze at the mention of my alcoholic father. Marcus glares at me with concerned eyes.

"Is that why you don't drink a lot?" Peter asks me.

I nod in response. "Also, about Hugo Danvers," I add. "That's one of the murders I don't regret doing." I look down at my now-folded arms on the table with a small grin.

Hearing someone snort, I look up. Peter tries to contain his laughter. "Come on," I say. "Go ahead and laugh. Danvers died a long time ago."

Marcus looks at him, his eyes slightly widened. "Excuse me?" he says with a questioning look. "Danvers was nice!"

Peter scoffs, rolling his eyes. "He was a real jerk!"

"He was not!"

"Yes, he was!"

"No, he was not!"

"Shut it! Both of you! Or I will break the doctor's arm and pull his eyeballs out of their sockets!" I threaten. I already know I won't do it. I just wanted them to shut up.

They did. They shut up in an instant. The sound of the doctor taking a step back echoes through the room. I chuckle slightly and hold up my hands. "Relax. Just shut up."

The man in the corner sighs in relief. Marcus clears his throat and orders the file. Peter runs a hand through his hair as he leans back in his chair.

They're not happy with my jokes.

Awkwardly, I clear my throat and straighten up. "Sorry," I apologize.

After about forty-five awkward minutes, the questioning ended. Marcus left the room and took the doctor with him, giving Peter and me the time to talk alone.

Peter smiles with his hands steepling. I smile widely and stand up. I gesture at him to do the same, which he does. He stands before me, his arms crossed over his chest.

I look at his tie and tighten it around his neck. I hear him scoff softly, his chest dropping as he does. His shoulders have lowered. He was stiff at the table during the questioning.

When I finish with his tie, I look up at him. "When you wear this tie," I tell him. "I want you to smile and think of the good times we had." I straighten his clip. "Not how crazy I was."

He takes my hands into his. Smiling reassuringly, he replies: "Of course. I promise I will."

I take a deep breath before my gaze goes over to his shoulders. He tilts his head with his smile widening slightly. "Want a hug?" he asks.

I nod twice before letting myself fall into his arms. I've missed him so much.

Burying my head into his shoulder, Peter gently strokes my back, whispering soothing words.

"When you leave through the door..." I softly say. "I may not see you for a long time..."

My eyes start watering at the thought of it.

I grasp his shirt and tighten the hug, feeling tears soaking his shoulder. He doesn't mind it. His gentle hands run through my hair as he rocks me back and forth.

"Everything will be alright," he tells me. "I will write."

"P-promise?" I ask, trying to contain my sobs.

I feel him a nod. "Yes. I promise."

Sobbing slightly, I nuzzle into his shoulder, taking in his scent one last time.

We let go.

Tears continue to stream down my face. I can't help but think of how it will be when he leaves.

I take a deep breath before asking: "Can you leave when I turn around? I don't want to see you leave."

He nods. A tear slides down his cheek. A sad smile tugs at the corner of his lips. A long inhale. "I'll miss you, Cheesecake."

"I'll miss you too, Pudding."

My feet feel like they're nailed to the ground, yet I managed to take a step back. I close my eyes and look down at the floor.

Footsteps.

Click.

Click.

The door shut.

EPILOGUE

Walking down the streets, I noticed that nothing really changed. Even after five years, it's still the same old town.

Early in the morning, the aromas of the different shops fill the air as I pass by. People who remembered me asked me how I was doing. I greeted them with a smile and told them the truth. I'm doing great.

I haven't heard from Peter in five months. I've always thought he'd been busy.

I entered the flower shop. It's a different florist.

She looks at me, and her smile fades. "John." She looks at me from top to toe. "How was your time in prison?"

I clench my jaw. Breathe. "Good seeing you again, Lily." I force a smile. "Also, I didn't go to prison. I went to a place where there were kind people, unlike you."

Lily scoffs and rolls her eyes. "You psychopath."

I laugh slightly. "They didn't have a stupid ass like you." I take a step closer. She frowns angrily. "They were kind, unlike you."

"How dare-"

"Shut. It." I step closer, towering over her. She gulps, and I see fear in her eyes. I'm not supposed to enjoy this, but I do. "You've been a bitch our whole relationship long. So. Shut. The. Fuck. Up."

The backdoor opens. The old florist enters the shop with a couple of boxes.

I smile genuinely at the man. "Good morning! It's been a long time," I greet him.

He smiles at me and replies: "Good morning, sir! It indeed has been a long time ago. How have you been?"

"I'm doing great, sir. Thank you."

"What would you like?" he asks me. "Nothing like stalking again, I hope."

I chuckle slightly. "No, no. That's over." I look around and take in the smell of freshly picked flowers. "Roses would be nice. Red and white."

The florist places the boxes on the counter and turns to Lily. "Will you help the man, or should I do it?"

Lily answers: "I'll help him. John and I have some things to discuss."

We both exchange glares. She breaks eye contact and walks right past me, her shoulder brushed against mine.

I let out a long sigh and followed her.

She points at the roses in white buckets. Carefully, I touch them, looking for a healthy flower for Peter.

"You're still a psychopath," Lily says.

I scoff and look over my shoulder. "You know..." I look back at the flowers. "...I could still break your arm with one swift move. You wouldn't want that, would you?"

She shakes her head quickly, her breath quickening. I grin at her fear. "What's this? Fear? Are you afraid of me?" I ask without looking at her.

"You're insane!" she shouts. "You're mental!"

I take out a dark red and a snow-white rose, ignoring Lily. I hold them under my nose, smelling the fresh aromas. "I'll take these two."

"Ribbon?"

I turn and see the man standing next to Lily. I smile at him. "You remembered." I look at the flowers. "I don't think I'll take a ribbon."

The florist nods with a friendly smile. "You know what? You can get them for free."

Surprised, I look up from the roses. "What?"

Lily looks surprised at the man.

"You can get them for free." He points at me. "You, my friend, have been through a lot. You just got out of a mental hospital or something. I'd like you to have a warm welcome."

A wide smile spreads across my face. "I don't know what to say." I chuckle slightly, rubbing the back of my neck. "Thank you!"

His warm smile widens. "It's almost nine o'clock. Go see your prince."

I look at my watch. "Oh!" I look at the door. "Thank you once again!"

With that said, I ran out of the shop. I ran toward the café, hoping that Peter would be there.

I pant as I reach the café. I look through the window, desperately searching for a glimpse of him.

There he was, sitting at a table, busy with his laptop.

Taking a deep breath, I enter the café.

I walk over to his table, thinking of what I could say.

There he was. One step. One word.

"Hey," I awkwardly say.

Peter looks up from his work and turns to me. His eyes widen, and his mouth opens as if he is trying to say something. He looks at me from top to toe, and I do the same with him.

He stands up from his chair, his eyes starting to tear. "Cheesecake...?" His voice cracked slightly. He doesn't hesitate. He jumps right at me, hugging me as tight as possible. I do the same, not wanting to let him go again.

We don't let go. I feel his tears wetting my shirt, but I don't mind it. I've missed him too much to care.

I take in his scent. His warmth. His touch. I want this moment to last forever. Having him in my embrace is everything.

We let go of each other and look each other in the eyes. Caressing his cheek, I wipe away his tears with my thumbs. We smile.

"H-how have you been?" Peter asks me, almost exploding with joy. "For how long have you been free? Were they nice? I'm sorry I stopped writing!"

I chuckle slightly and hug him again. "I missed you too, Pudding."

He nuzzles his head into my neck, causing me to whisper: "You're the adorable one."

He grunts softly and replies: "Shut it..."

We let go of each other once again.

I look down at his shirt. He's wearing the tie and clip. His smile widens as he sees me looking at them. "I always wear them to work. People started asking me why I kept wearing it every day..."

I smile widely and mess up his hair. I focus on his tie once again and tighten it. "You need to know how to tighten a tie, Pudding," I tell him, straightening his clip. "This must be the second time I'm doing this."

He laughs, shaking his head. His gaze falls upon the door.

"John," I hear a familiar voice say. His strong accent betrays him.

I swallow hard before turning around. I haven't seen them in so long. They only visited twice.

Juliette steps closer. I lower my gaze, not daring to look at them.

"Idiota." She grabs my arm and pulls me toward her. I freeze once she does it, not knowing how to react. Finally, I close my arms around her, hugging her back.

"Eres un idiota. (You're an idiot.)" She takes a step back. "Pero sigue siendo mi hermanito. (But still my little brother.)"

I smile slightly and press my lips against her forehead, whispering: "Te quiero, hermana. (I love you, sister.)"

I turn to José. Juliette steps to Peter, giving us the space.

"Hermano." I nod once, greeting him. "Good seeing you again."

He steps toward me, his steps echoing through the now-quiet café. I lower my head, scared that he might hit me again.

"Fuck it," I hear him say. Just like I expected, he hit me. But then he hugged me tightly, surprising me. My breath hitches as I don't know how to react. We haven't hugged in so long.

He pulls away. "You may be an ass, but you're our ass."

"Family of asses!" Juliette shouts.

Peter snorts, trying to contain his laughter, but ends up laughing anyway. I missed hearing his laugh.

Peter and I left the café. He has a suitcase because he has his laptop with him. We talk about how it has been in these five years separated.

He has new cases to do and has a new enemy at the workplace who he calls Stinky Dumb Dumb. That's a weird name, I know, but it's hilarious.

I told him about how nice the doctors were. I made new friends in group therapy.

"Hey, Peter?" I ask. "Can I ask you a question?"

He looks at me. "Oh? You used my name. What's wrong?"

"I'm not forcing you to answer me."

"Go ahead, John."

We stop at a stop light. I take a deep breath. "What did you think of that night?"

The light turns green, yet we don't walk. He looks at me. I'm not sure what emotions he's feeling. His expressions don't say anything.

I gulp and shake my head. "Nevermind. Let's keep going."

As soon as I want to take a step, Peter says: "I enjoyed it."

I freeze, not daring to look at him. "What?"

"I may have wanted it to stop, but I somehow enjoyed it."

Speechless, I look at him, not knowing what to say. He shrugs and gestures to the other side before walking. I stay still for a moment, thinking about it before following.

"W-wait!" I shout after him. "You liked it?"

He nods in response. "Years ago, I didn't want to talk about it because Marcus was there."

We reach the police station. I can't enter it anymore without having something to rapport.

I look at Peter, who looks back at me. "See you again later?" I ask.

He sighs and shakes his head. "Fieldwork today." He looks at his watch. "Marcus could be here any moment."

"Hey, douchebag! Who's your trash bag?" a male voice shouts at us.

I see Peter's jaw tighten as he forces a smile. "Liam Smith," he mumbles. He turns around, and I do the same. An annoying-looking cop stands behind us with some shades on even though it's fall.

"Sup, dickhead!" He bumps Peter's shoulder. "I swear, you'll be dead by the end of the mission!"

I feel the heat rising between the two. With myself, I feel an urge to protect Peter.

Liam turns to me and examinates me. "You look weak," he says. "Punch me, nerd."

I shake my head. "Oh, I'm sorry. No hablo con idiotas como tú. (I don't speak to idiots like you.)"

His smirk fades. "Oh, an Italian freak."

The anger begins to boil inside me. Blood pumps through my veins as the temptation of punching this guy in the face increases.

"He's not Italian," Peter says. "You're just an idiot who can't see the difference between people-"

"I can see the difference between myself and other people!" he argues. "I'm better than other people!"

"Do you look into a mirror?" I ask him.

He turns to me. "What?"

"Do you look into a mirror?" I repeat.

"Of course I do."

I scoff. "Did your mirror break into pieces when you looked at it?"

"How dare-"

"Good that mirrors can't talk or laugh. You'd be depressed for decades."

"Take tha-"

"Such a shame I don't have glasses. I would've taken them off already because you're too ugly to look at."

"Oh, you bitch!"

I start to laugh. "Oh, yes! Mama raised a bitch and not a moron like you!"

He tries to hit me, but I stop his punch. He tries pulling away, but I keep his fist in my grasp. "You snail." I get near his face with anger burning in my eyes. "Fuck. Off."

I hear him gulp, and I let go of his fist. He looks at Peter, opening his mouth, but shuts it right after. He glares at me once again before hurrying inside.

Grinning widely, I look at Peter. He looks surprised. "You did not just tell Smith fuck off in that way."

I shrug and wink at him. "Maybe I did."

I hear someone clapping. I turn around and see Marcus smiling widely.

"Marcus!" I say, smiling too. "It's so good to see you!"

"Amazing seeing you too, John." He holds out his hand, and I shake it. "How is everything going? I see that you made a new friend."

I scoff and roll my eyes. "Oh, that. That's nothing compared to what I can really do." I wink at Peter.

His lips thinned as he looked away, his cheeks slightly flushed.

Marcus chuckles and shakes his head. "You two..." He has files with him, and I see a gun in a holster underneath his jacket. "What do you see? Hear? Feel?"

"I see your gun in a holster. Glock 19." I examine him further. "Files about a triple murder." I snort slightly. "Hope you had fun with your wife."

Peter bursts out in laughter as I say my last words. Marcus's nose ruffles up as he frowns, his cheeks a bit pink from embarrassment.

"W-wait!" Peter tries to calm himself down. "How did you guess all that?"

I shrug. "That's something I have as an ex-stalker. I have a good eye." I point at the file. "Three yellow sticky notes for the three victims and a blue one for the murderer." I point at his jacket. "I can see your holster with the gun." I point at his shirt's collar. "And there we have a lipstick stain."

Marcus grunts slightly. "You're good."

"Very."

I smirk, visibly enjoying this.

Marcus pats Peter's shoulder. "I'll see you inside." He turns to me. "Don't do anything illegal and keep yourself in."

I roll my eyes. "As if I would do anything bad."

Marcus raises both eyebrows, reminding me of what I just did to Liam. "Relax! He's not dead, and I won't kill or punch anyone."

Marcus nods once before entering the building, leaving Peter and I alone on the streets.

"What did you see when you were stalking me?" Peter suddenly asks.

I press my lips together, not really wanting to tell the truth. I sigh and run a hand through my hair as I smile awkwardly. "Well... I know how you look naked. I have pictures and videos."

His eyes widen slightly as a frown forms at the same time. I lick my lips wet, not knowing what else to say.

He sighs. "I catch myself thinking about that one night." I look at him. He looks down at his shoes. "Whenever I do, I can't help but question how it would feel if we did it again."

I clench my jaw and form trembling fists. I shut my eyes tightly. I can already imagine it. Him being tied down, begging for more, moaning for more. I try to shake away the thoughts but can't help but think of more. "Oh, Peter... You're a curse for me..."

He chuckles slightly. He takes my hand, and I try to pull away, thinking that I might not be able to hold back. He smiles slightly. "Don't hold back," he whispers.

I groan at the fact that I don't want to do anything else. "Fuck it." I push him against the wall and pin his arms above his head, causing his suitcase to drop. Leaning forward, causing our faces to be inches apart, I say: "Your choice."

"Go ahead."

I kiss him.

I.

Kiss.

Him.

He kisses me back. It's better than I could have imagined. His lips are soft, the warmth of his breath hits my skin, and he kisses me back.

I slide my tongue between his lips and let our tongues intertwine with each other. I feel his knees buckle slightly.

I never imagined our first kiss to be this rough.

We pull away, leaving a thin thread of saliva connecting our lips. His breath is shallow, and his eyes are filled with love.

That look in his eyes. I will never forget it.

"Hey, Peter! You coming?" we hear Marcus shout.

I curse under my breath, not wanting this moment to end. I may have wanted that hug from before to last forever, but this was the one thing I wanted to last forever and ever and relive it over and over again.

I step back, preventing myself from doing anything else. For now.

Peter leans against the wall, his chest rising and dropping with every shallow pant. A smile spreads across his face. "That was amazing," he says breathlessly.

I grin mischievously and kiss his forehead. I get near his ear. "Later tonight," I whisper seductively. "When I get to your place, I want to find you on your knees in your bedroom." I lick his ear and blow it slightly. I see the goosebumps on his skin. I nod at the door. "Go ahead."

He gulps and takes a step to the door. I hear an audible sigh as he turns around. "One last kiss?" he asks with such an innocent tone.

I scoff and take a step toward him. I grab the back of his neck and kiss him passionately.

We pull away.

"You're greedy," I tell him, chuckling slightly.

"Says the stalker."

"Ex-stalker."

"Yeah, yeah."

"Go on. The faster you go, the faster you're finished, the faster we can have our fun."

Peter smiles and shakes his head. "Of course..." He turns to the door and opens it. "See you tonight, Cheesecake!" he says without looking over his shoulder as he walks inside. I grin slightly, realizing he hasn't realized the flowers in his belt loops.

I sigh deeply with joy. I look up at the cloudy sky and watch as leaves fly by. "Such a good day..."

9 781934 232545